LUCENT LIBRARY OF
BLACK HISTORY

UNSUNG
HEROES Women of the Civil Rights Movement

By Jennifer Lombardo

Portions of this book originally appeared in
Women Civil Rights Leaders by Anne Wallace Sharp.

LUCENT
P R E S S

Published in 2020 by
Lucent Press, an Imprint of Greenhaven Publishing, LLC
353 3rd Avenue
Suite 255
New York, NY 10010

Designer: Deanna Paternostro
Editor: Jennifer Lombardo

MAR 1 3 2020

Cataloging-in-Publication Data

Names: Lombardo, Jennifer.
Title: Unsung heroes: women of the civil rights movement / Jennifer Lombardo.
Description: New York : Lucent Press, 2020. | Series: Lucent library of black history | Includes index.
Identifiers: ISBN 9781534568686 (pbk.) | ISBN 9781534568655 (library bound) | ISBN 9781534568624
(ebook)
Subjects: LCSH: Women civil rights workers–United States–History–20th century–Juvenile literature. |
African American women civil rights workers–History–20th century–Juvenile literature. | Civil rights
movements–United States–History–20th century–Juvenile literature. | Women civil rights workers–United
States–Biography–Juvenile literature. | African American women civil rights workers–Biography–
Juvenile literature.
Classification: LCC E185.61 L66 2020 | DDC 323.092'2 B–dc23

Printed in China

Some of the images in this book illustrate individuals who are models. The depictions do not imply
actual situations or events.

CPSIA compliance information: Batch #BW20KL: For further information contact Greenhaven Publishing LLC, New York, New York at 1-844-317-7404.

Please visit our website, www.greenhavenpublishing.com. For a free color catalog of all our
high-quality books, call toll free 1-844-317-7404 or fax 1-844-317-7405.

CONTENTS

FOREWORD

From medicine and law to sports and literature, African Americans have played a major role in the history of the United States. However, these groundbreaking men and women often faced prejudice and persecution. More than 300 years ago, Africans were taken in chains from their home and enslaved to work for the earliest American settlers. They suffered for more than two centuries under the brutal oppression of their owners until the outbreak of the American Civil War in 1861. After the dust settled four years later and thousands of Americans—both black and white—had died in combat, slavery in the United States had been legally abolished. By the turn of the 20th century, with the help of the 13th, 14th, and 15th Amendments to the U.S. Constitution, African American men had finally won significant battles for the basic rights of citizenship, but the fight for equality was far from over. Even after the successes of the civil rights movement, the struggle continued—and it still continues today.

Although the history of the African American experience is not always a pleasant story, it is also filled with powerful moments of positive change. These triumphs of human equality were achieved with help from brave social activists such as Frederick Douglass, Martin Luther King Jr., and Maya Angelou. They all experienced racial prejudice in their lifetimes and fought by writing, speaking, and acting against it. By exposing the suffering of the black community, they brought people together to try to remedy centuries' worth of wrongdoing.

Today, it is important to learn about the history of African Americans and their experiences in modern America in order to work toward healing the divide that still exists in the United States. This series aims to give readers a deeper appreciation for and understanding of a part of the American story that is often left untold.

Even before the legal emancipation of slaves, black culture was thriving despite many attempts to suppress it. From music to language to art, slaves began cultivating an identity that was completely unique. Soon after these slaves were granted citizenship, African American culture burst into the mainstream. New generations of authors, scholars, painters, and singers were born, and they spread an appreciation for black culture across America and the entire world. Studying the contributions of these talented individuals fosters a sense of optimism. Despite the cruel treatment and racist attitudes these men and women faced, they never gave up, and they helped change the world with their determination and unique voices.

The Lucent Library of Black History offers a glimpse into the lives and accomplishments of some of the most important and influential African Americans across historical time periods and areas of interest. From the arts and sports to the military and politics, the wide variety of topics allows readers to get a full and clear picture of the successes and struggles African Americans have experienced and are continuing to experience. Titles examine primary source documents and quotes from historical and modern figures to provide an enriching learning experience for readers. With detailed timelines, unique sidebars, and a carefully selected bibliography for further research, this series gives readers the tools to independently discover historical events and figures that do not often get their time in the spotlight.

By balancing the harsh realities of the past and present with a sense of hopefulness for the future, the Lucent Library of Black History helps young people understand an essential truth: Black history is a vital part of American history.

SETTING THE SCENE:

1957
Dorothy Height is elected president of the National Council of Negro Women and holds the position for 40 years; Daisy Bates mentors the Little Rock Nine as they integrate Central High School.

1940
Ella Baker becomes the field secretary for the NAACP and begins organizing youth chapters.

1892
The People's Grocery lynchings take place, prompting Ida B. Wells to start her anti-lynching crusade.

| 1892 | 1896 | 1940 | 1955 | 1956 | 1957 | 1960 |

1896
The National Association of Colored Women's Clubs is founded after Josephine St. Pierre Ruffin issues a call for black women to band together.

1955
Rosa Parks refuses to give up her seat on a Montgomery bus on December 1; Jo Ann Gibson Robinson organizes a yearlong, citywide bus boycott beginning on December 5.

1956
Septima Clark takes a job at the Highlander Folk School teaching literacy and citizenship skills.

1960
Dorothy Height becomes the first woman to join the Taconic Foundation, a group dedicated to furthering civil and human rights; SNCC is created and urged by Ella Baker to remain an independent organization.

A TIMELINE

1961
After the Highlander Folk School is shut down, Septima Clark begins working with SCLC to establish Citizenship Schools.

1964
Fannie Lou Hamer helps found the Mississippi Freedom Democratic Party and organizes a black delegation to challenge the all-white delegation at the Democratic National Convention, where she makes a televised speech about her experience at the Winona jail.

| 1961 | 1963 | 1964 | 1965 | 2011 |

1963
Fannie Lou Hamer and six others are brutally beaten at a jail in Winona, Mississippi.

1965
Amelia Boynton is knocked unconscious during the march from Selma to Montgomery.

2011
Kimberly Bryant founds Black Girls Code to help black girls advance in technology classes.

INTRODUCTION

WOMEN'S WORK

When people think about the civil rights movement of the 1950s and 1960s, it is likely that they immediately think of Martin Luther King Jr., the preacher who was the public face of the civil rights movement. Many people also likely call to mind Malcolm X, who advocated a less peaceful approach to the goal of giving black men and women rights equal to those white people enjoyed. While these two men were instrumental in helping black people achieve civil rights, many black women were equally influential. In fact, the civil rights movement, according to historian Lynne Olson, "was a struggle that women helped to mold, lead, and organize from its very beginning."[1]

Starting with the abolitionist movement to end slavery in the 19th century, black women have championed many efforts to end racial injustice. They have worked to end lynching (killing someone for an accused crime without a proper legal trial), have fought for fair housing, and have protested discrimination and prejudice wherever they found it. Black women, in fact, participated at every level of the civil rights movement. Those who assumed leadership roles, however, were often overlooked and given little credit for their efforts. For example, even today, many children learn in school that Rosa Parks, the woman who helped start the Montgomery bus boycott, refused to move to the back of the bus because she had worked a long day and was tired. This implies that her involvement in the civil rights movement was accidental. In reality, Parks's action was a calculated act of civil disobedience, and she was so influential that some have called her the "Mother of the Freedom Movement."

Although Parks made it into the history books, hundreds of women in the civil rights movement were not well-known, either then or now. The majority were volunteers, such as the hundreds of church women who prepared meals, cleaned up after meetings, and marched silently and anonymously. These women went door-to-door working for voter registration, housed and fed white activists, and passed out leaflets and other information. Unita Blackwell, a former sharecropper and one of Mississippi's most effective organizers, once said, "Who's the people that really keeps things going on? It's women ... So in the black community the movement quite naturally emerged out of all the women."[2]

Hundreds of these women played small but significant roles in the fight for equality. Joanne Christian, for instance, was a 14-year-old who walked

Women were an instrumental part of the civil rights movement but were often not given credit for their participation.

the streets of Albany, Georgia, convincing black people to register to vote. For her efforts, she was arrested 13 times. Clara Luper was an Oklahoma civil rights activist who led a sit-in at a drugstore lunch counter in Oklahoma City; her actions helped lead to the integration of lunch counters in Oklahoma, Missouri, Kansas, and Iowa.

Big Responsibility, Little Credit

The actions taken by the women of the civil rights movement were often either downplayed or outright ignored. The media focused primarily on such leaders as King, who, along with other black ministers, often marginalized women's efforts. Even when women did achieve leadership positions, there was never a sense of equal partnership with the men of the movement. Historian Jacqueline A. Rouse explained, "Women in positions where they demonstrated important leadership skills often were not given the formal titles, nor the respect, their work deserved ... Women's activities did not fit the traditional definition of leadership."[3]

King and the other male leaders of the civil rights movement were viewed as leaders because of their positions as heads of various civil rights organizations. They were often seen as figureheads who were highly visible in the media but did not do much of the hands-on work themselves. For women, on the other hand, the opposite was generally true. With the exception of Dorothy Height, who was the president of the National Council of Negro Women, none of the major female figures in the civil rights movement served as important figureheads for specific groups. Instead, they worked behind the scenes, setting an example for others to follow.

Part of the reason women often were not recognized as leaders was a mindset that was common during the early 20th century and the civil rights era of the 1950s and 1960s. Although women had been advocating for equal rights since the late 19th century, very few advances had been made by the time of the civil rights movement. Men were expected to be the leaders, both at home and in the workplace. Women were expected to be their helpers, not their equals.

Reversing a Trend

Female civil rights leaders were also often ignored by the historians who wrote books about the civil rights movement. The last two decades, however, have seen a reversal of the tendency to disregard the contributions of women, with more historians looking into the

In the 1950s and 1960s, white and black women alike were expected to stay behind the scenes, quietly serving the men in their lives. However, many women went against this expectation and achieved great things.

accomplishments of female civil rights activists—even those who did not have leadership roles. For instance, Septima Clark helped educate the black masses about their rights and how to vote, and Fannie Lou Hamer was instrumental not only in organizing grassroots protests in Mississippi but also in helping to found a political party. Clark, through her work with various civil rights organizations, spent most of her adult life working to improve the lives of her fellow African Americans through education. Hamer played her greatest role during Freedom Summer in 1964. Leading by example, Hamer's courage and determination brought thousands of black citizens into the civil rights movement. She was also instrumental in the creation of the Mississippi Freedom Democratic Party, a party that challenged the all-white

Mississippi Democratic Party at the 1964 Democratic Convention.

These formerly unknown women, as well as many others, played essential roles in the civil rights movement. Civil rights activist and former ambassador to the United Nations Andrew Young noted, "It was the … uncommon black people of the South who, year after year, through their dedication and sacrifices made the southern civil rights movement possible. They were not the publicized leaders of the media … but they were the core of the movement."[4]

CHAPTER ONE
FIGHTING TO END LYNCHING

For years, black people—especially those in the South—lived in constant fear of lynching. Lynching is different than murder because it is the attempt of a mob of people to take the law into their own hands. A murder can occur for any reason; a lynch mob, in contrast, would first accuse someone of a crime and then kill them for that crime, generally by hanging them. However, it is important to note that just because someone was accused of a crime did not mean they had committed it. Many people who were lynched were innocent. The ones who were guilty in the eyes of the law had generally broken laws that were unfair, such as one that enforced segregation (the forced separation of black and white people).

According to the National Association for the Advancement of Colored People (NAACP), lynching became common after the American Civil War ended and was used by whites as a way to punish freed blacks for "getting away with too much freedom."[5] Many white people did not like to think that black people were equal to them and wanted to make sure they remained too scared to act like anything other than second-class citizens. Between 1882 and 1968, 4,743 lynchings were recorded, although it is highly likely that many more took place and were not recorded at all. Of those, 3,446, or about 73 percent, were directed at black people. White people were also lynched, but it was a much less common occurrence and, according to the NAACP, generally happened to people who tried to stop the practice of lynching or to help black people improve their lives. Ida B. Wells—also known by her married name, Wells-Barnett—was one black woman who made it her mission to help end the threat of lynching. Crusading in both the United States

Many lynchings were carried out by hanging. Shown here is an anti-lynching protest.

and abroad, Wells risked her life to make Americans and others aware of the horrifying nature of lynching and the reasons behind it.

A Born Fighter

Ida Bell Wells was born a slave in 1862 in Holly Springs, Mississippi. Following the death of her parents, Wells helped raise her brothers and sisters. In 1882, she and her two youngest sisters moved to Memphis, Tennessee, to live with an aunt. While there, Wells passed a test that would allow her to become a city school teacher. When her aunt and younger sisters moved to California, Wells remained in Memphis, living in a series of boardinghouses and rented rooms while she attended college part-time at Fisk University in Nashville.

In 1884, Wells bought a first-class train ticket in Memphis, Tennessee, to the school where she taught classes in Woodstock, Tennessee. The train conductor asked her to leave the first-class car so white passengers would not have

SPEAKING OUT AGAINST SLAVERY

Ida B. Wells was not the first black woman to risk her life to speak out against issues that affected black people. Isabella Baumfree, also known as Belle, was one of 12 children in a family of slaves who were owned by several different plantation owners in the state of New York. When slavery was outlawed in that state in 1827, Baumfree's owner refused to free her. Rather than accept his decision, Belle took her youngest son and fled to New York City.

Years later, motivated by a religious vision, the 46-year-old Baumfree left her home in New York City and set forth across the country with no more than 25 cents in her pocket. She changed her name to Sojourner Truth because she wanted to travel from place to place and tell everyone the truth about slavery. ("Sojourn" is another word for "journey.") Standing six feet tall, Truth had a strong and powerful voice that often mesmerized her audiences. Despite being physically beaten for speaking out against slavery, Truth never gave up her campaign. In 1850, she dictated her life story to a white friend. Another friend, abolitionist and journalist William Lloyd Garrison, arranged for the publication of the story, titled *The Narrative of Sojourner Truth*.

Following the end of the Civil War, Truth worked for the Freedmen's Bureau, helping the newly freed slaves get an education, find work, and locate housing. She dedicated the last decades of her life to opening the doors of freedom for all people, especially former slaves and women. Long before the 1960s, Sojourner Truth was leading the fight for civil rights.

to sit with a black person. She would have to move to the crowded and dirty smoking car, where passengers could smoke cigars and cigarettes; the smoking car also served as the "Negro" car.

Wells refused to leave her seat, pointing out that she had purchased a first-class ticket. She was then forcibly removed from the seat by several men, but she fought back. Wells later wrote of the incident in her memoirs:

He [the conductor] tried to drag me out of the seat, but the moment he caught hold of my arm, I fastened my teeth in the back of his hand. I had braced my feet against the back of the seat in front and was holding to the back ... He went forward and got the baggage man and another man to help him and, of course, they succeeded in dragging me out. They were encouraged to do this by the attitude of the white ladies and gentlemen of the car; some of them stood on the seats so they could get a good view and continued applauding the conductor for his brave stand.[6]

Wells was enraged and humiliated by these actions and left the train at the next stop. She hired an attorney to file a lawsuit based on an 1881 Tennessee law that required separate but equal accommodations on trains; she argued that the smoking car was not at all equal to the first-class car she had been forced to leave. Wells sued the railroad and was awarded $200 in compensation by a Memphis judge. The railroad filed an appeal, and the earlier judgment was overturned in 1887 by the state supreme court. The judges argued that the accommodations provided for black people were, in fact, equal in comfort and safety.

Writing About Social Issues

Following the Tennessee Supreme Court decision, a black church newspaper asked Wells to write an article about the incident on the train, the lawsuit, and the inequity of the law. In this article, she emphasized that black people needed to stand up for their rights, and her message was so well received that a number of other black newspapers and magazines asked her to write columns and articles for them. Wells was soon able to earn a respectable living through her writing.

By 1888, Wells was contributing to black newspapers across the country. Often writing under the pen name "Iola" to protect her identity, Wells met and networked with editors and journalists throughout the country. In 1889, she became a full partner in a local Memphis black newspaper, the *Free Speech and Headlight*. Her intention was to write for the thousands of ordinary citizens who wanted to be informed about current events. Wells explained, "I had an instinctive feeling that people who have little or no school training should have something coming into their homes weekly which dealt with their problems in a simple, helpful way ... so I wrote in a plain, common-sense way on the things that concerned our people."[7]

In addition to her success with writing, Wells also continued to teach in the Memphis school system. In the late 1880s, however, she wrote an

Ida B. Wells wrote many articles encouraging black people to stand up for the rights they deserved.

school board of being racist. The school system responded by not renewing Wells's teaching contract.

A Tragic Event

By the early 1890s, Wells was a well-known member of the black community in Memphis. Two of her closest friends were Thomas Moss and his wife. Moss was among a group of black people who opened the People's Grocery, a store intended to compete for black customers with a white-owned grocery store in the same neighborhood. Violence soon broke out between clerks at the two stores. Despite both sides being involved, only the black clerks were charged with the crime of starting a riot.

editorial in the paper criticizing the school system. During this time, black students were forced to go to school in broken-down buildings that did not have heat, water, or proper desks. They often sat on uncomfortable benches, used outdated textbooks, relied on teachers without the proper training, and walked miles to and from school. Wells called these conditions disgraceful and shameful and accused the

Following the arrests, rumors quickly circulated through Memphis that black citizens were preparing to attack white businesses. The police were sent to arrest black people who had not been involved in the initial riot, resulting in the outbreak of further violence. There was shooting and vandalism in the black community, which led to the arrest of many well-known black

Today, interracial couples similar to this one are not uncommon. However, in the past, it was illegal for black and white people to date. In particular, black men who were seen with white women were in danger of being accused of rape and lynched.

whites looted the People's Grocery and destroyed the store.

This triple murder is an example of a lynching because the men were first accused of a crime and were executed by a group, commonly called a "lynch mob." Despite the fact that the members of lynch mobs were generally well-known to the police and the white community, few were ever arrested. The police, as well as local politicians in the South, overlooked the crime of lynching and occasionally participated in the murders themselves. The white press praised the efforts of the men who committed this crime, believing that they were ridding the community of threats.

The press often used the protection of white women as the justification for lynching, claiming that the black men were guilty of raping white women. However, the NAACP noted that rape "was not a great factor in reasoning behind the lynching. It was the third greatest cause of lynchings behind homicides and 'all

people, including Thomas Moss. While Moss and several other blacks were housed in the Memphis jail, a group of whites, led by law enforcement officers, entered the jail and seized three black men, including Moss. All were taken out of the jail to a rural area and shot to death. While this was happening, other

other causes.'"[8]

In truth, Moss and other black businessmen had only threatened the profits of a white business. Throughout the South, whites were reacting violently to any evidence of black financial success. In fact, the South's economic and social system depended on keeping black people in an inferior status. White Southerners were so afraid of black people succeeding that many of them were willing to commit violent crimes to prevent this from happening.

Moss's death was a turning point for Wells. When no one was punished or arrested for the murder of her friend, Wells was outraged. She wrote, "This is what opened my eyes to what lynching really was: an excuse to get rid of Negroes who were acquiring wealth and property."[9] She took immediate action: Following the murders, Wells started her crusade to end lynching.

Risking Her Safety

Wells's criticism of lynching was fierce and angered whites throughout the South. She was also highly critical of well-known black leaders for their inaction. In an editorial, or opinion column, she called on black leaders in Memphis and the state of Tennessee to act, writing, "Where are our 'leaders' when the race is being burnt, shot, and hanged? ... 'Our leaders' make no demands on the country to protect us, nor come forward with any practical plan for changing the condition of affairs."[10]

In addition to writing articles, Wells also started a thorough investigation of the practice of lynching. She traveled throughout the South, talking to family members of victims and people who had witnessed the crimes, documenting more than 700 lynchings that had occurred in the 1890s. In the process, she became the target of a lynch mob herself and received numerous death threats. For instance, in one editorial in the *Free Speech* newspaper, Wells debunked the myth that black men were raping white women. This excuse, she stated, was often made by white Southerners to defend lynching. She used statistics gathered through careful research to back up her statements. The white community in Memphis was furious that Wells had insulted white women by claiming that they were liars. While Wells was out of town, a white mob stormed her newspaper office and burned it to the ground. Her friends warned her not to return to Memphis, so Wells never set foot in the city again.

Not Stopping

The destruction of her newspaper office did not discourage Wells. Remaining in New York, she wrote for several

RAISING A FUSS

The daughter of two former slaves, Mary Church Terrell dedicated her life to fighting for civil and women's rights. After graduating from Oberlin College in Ohio in 1884, she became a teacher at Wilberforce College, also in Ohio. She later married a judge, Robert Terrell, and moved to Washington, D.C., where she was appointed to the city's board of education—the first black woman in the United States to hold such a position.

After a friend of hers in Memphis, Tennessee, was killed by a lynch mob in 1892 in the same incident that caused Ida B. Wells to take action, Terrell demanded a meeting with President Benjamin Harrison. The president agreed to meet with her and leading black advocate Frederick Douglass. Harrison heard their impassioned plea for a law to address lynching but took no action. It was this inaction that caused Terrell to dedicate the remainder of her life to fighting racism.

In 1896, she helped form the National Association of Colored Women, an organization dedicated to improving the lives of black women. She traveled throughout the South, speaking about the achievements of black women, and wrote numerous articles highlighting civil rights issues. In 1940, she wrote and published her autobiography, *A Colored Woman in a White World*, describing the prejudice and discrimination she had encountered throughout her life. She wrote, "As a colored woman, I may walk from the Capitol to the White House, ravenously hungry and abundantly supplied with money ... without finding a single restaurant in which I would be permitted to take a morsel of food."[1]

Terrell continued fighting her entire life. At the age of 86, she headed the Coordinating Committee for the Enforcement of the District of Columbia Anti-Discrimination Laws. She led meetings, spoke at rallies, and organized a protest at Thompson's Cafeteria in Washington, D.C. When she and her fellow activists were asked to leave the segregated restaurant, she and the committee filed a lawsuit. While the case was being decided, Terrell led the picket line day after day in front of the cafeteria. On June 8, 1953—one year before Terrell's death—the Supreme Court ordered the end of racial segregation in the District of Columbia.

1. Quoted in Lynne Olson, *Freedom's Daughters: The Unsung Heroines of the Civil Rights Movement from 1830 to 1970.* New York, NY: Simon & Schuster, 2001, p. 76.

publications, including the *New York Age*, a black newspaper. She continued to write articles condemning lynching. For instance, in 1898, Wells wrote in an article for the *Cleveland Gazette*:

> *For nearly twenty years lynching crimes ... have been committed and permitted by this Christian nation. Nowhere in the civilized world, save the United States of America, do men, possessing all civil and political power, go out in a band of 50 to 5,000 to hunt down, shoot, hang, or burn to death a single individual unarmed and absolutely powerless ... We refuse to believe that a country, so powerful to defend its citizens abroad, is unable to protect its citizens at home.*[11]

Wells was not the only woman to work to end lynching. Mary Burnett Talbert was another influential leader on this issue. Born and raised in Oberlin, Ohio, she later moved to Little Rock, Arkansas, and became a teacher. In 1887, she was given the job of assistant principal of Union High School in Little Rock; at the time, this was the highest office held by a black woman in the entire state of Arkansas. In 1891, she married and moved to Buffalo, New York. According to the National Women's Hall of Fame, Talbert "was a founding member of the Phyllis Wheatley Club, the first in Buffalo to affiliate with the National Association of Colored Women's Clubs. The Club established a settlement house and helped organize the first chapter of the NAACP"[12] in 1910. She became the president of the National Association of Colored Women and, under her leadership, the association became "a truly national institution with structure and organizational procedures."[13]

Talbert, like Wells, was outspoken against lynching. She was the driving force behind the Dyer Anti-Lynching Bill, which was introduced to Congress in 1918 and aimed to set harsher punishments for lynching. The bill passed the House of Representatives in 1918 but failed in the Senate due to powerful southern senators who voted against it. No law was ever passed by Congress to ban lynching specifically, although today, anyone who commits this crime can be charged with murder.

During an era when lynch mobs were common and black deaths were numerous, only a few brave people were willing to speak out against these atrocities. The actions of Wells, Talbert, and other leaders to bring attention to the issue caused the number of lynchings to decrease dramatically. As time went on and the political and social

Shown here are members of the Phyllis Wheatley Club of Buffalo, New York,
including Mary Burnett Talbert (standing, fourth from left).

climate changed, lynching became much less of a threat than it had been in the past.

Lynching in the 21st Century

Thanks to the efforts of anti-lynching crusaders, lynching generally does not occur anymore. Public opinion has moved away from openly supporting people who commit this crime to viewing them as the criminals they truly are. While the murder of black people does, sadly, still happen frequently, the days when a lynch mob might show up on someone's front lawn at any time to kill them for a crime they did not commit are generally over. However, threats of lynching still linger. For example, in 2015, a student at Berkeley High School in California threatened to host a public lynching. Although he did not intend to carry out his threat, he did intend to cause extreme fear in the black student population—and he succeeded. About 1,500 Berkeley high school students walked out of their classes on November 5, the day the student behind the threats confessed, and protested on the University of California, Berkeley, campus to make a statement about the way the lynching threat had affected them.

Lynching is still sometimes discussed in the media, but some people have criticized others for using the term too loosely. For example, in an article for *Rolling Stone* magazine in February 2019, senior writer Jamil Smith noted that some black men who have committed real crimes have used the phrase "lynching" as a way to try to gain sympathy and deflect the accusations against them. Smith wrote, "Though many argue that lynchings continue, some evolving into reckless police killings, the metaphor remains too casually employed. It is utterly inapplicable even in cases of libel and slander. The insult to the thousands who died this way grows exponentially with every instance of exaggeration."[14] He cited actor Bill Cosby, recording artist R. Kelly, and Justin Fairfax, the lieutenant governor of Virginia, as examples. All three men have been accused of rape or sexual assault, and while only Cosby has been found guilty as of August 2019, many people say the evidence has shown that the other two are likely guilty as well. However, all three have referred to their trials and accusations as modern-day lynching—a comparison Smith and others believe shows a cruel disregard for the people who were killed by actual lynch mobs.

When it comes to violence against black people that has real comparisons to lynching, black activists, like their predecessors, are refusing to remain silent. For example, in January 2019, two black senators—Kamala Harris of California and Cory Booker of New Jersey—co-sponsored a bill called the Justice for Victims of Lynching Act that would make lynching a federal hate crime. This action shows that black leaders are still unafraid to make their voices heard when it comes to fighting injustice.

CHAPTER TWO
ORGANIZATIONS FOR BLACK WOMEN

One of the most powerful tools activists have is the ability to organize. One person alone is limited in the amount they can do, but when people with similar views come together to support each other, their impact is magnified. Over the years, many organizations have been founded that allow black women to combine their talents and create real, lasting change.

One such organization was the National Council of Negro Women, which was led by activist Dorothy Height until she stepped down as president in 1997 at the age of 85. Episcopal bishop Thomas L. Hoyt, in presenting Height an award in 2004 on behalf of the National Council of Churches, praised Height for her years of activism. He summarized her importance to the civil rights movement by saying, "She is a living legend in the movement for civil rights in this nation. She has dedicated herself to improving the quality of life for African American women and children. She is known internationally for her work for human rights for all. The world is truly a better place because of the work ... of Dr. Dorothy Irene Height."[15]

A Family Legacy

Height was born in Richmond, Virginia, on March 24, 1912. She and her family moved to Rankin, Pennsylvania, when she was four years old. At the time, many black people were moving north in search of jobs.

Height's father was a self-employed building contractor, and her mother was active in the Pennsylvania Federation of Colored Women's Clubs. Journalist Lea E. Williams explained that clubs such as these "began forming in the late 19th century to counter negative stereotypes, decry lynching and Jim Crow [segregation] laws, combat the woeful neglect of black

This photo of Height was taken in the 1960s, after she followed her mother's example and became active in black women's organizations.

New York's Barnard College but was refused entry because it had already met its quota of black students. She was accepted instead at New York University, where she obtained her bachelor's and master's degrees, majoring in educational psychology.

Height's first job was as a social worker for the United Christian Youth Movement, investigating the problems of young people. In the mid-1930s, she became an officer in the National Youth Council and fought discrimination wherever she found it. She later wrote, "Thanks to the national youth movement, I was actively engaged in helping to shape the agenda that set the goals for which I struggled for many years: laws to prevent lynching, the breakdown of segregation in the armed forces, free access to public accommodations, equal opportunity in education and employment ... an end to bias and discrimination."[18]

women's health and well-being, and support black women's suffrage."[16] In her autobiography, Height described attending many of these meetings with her mother. She wrote, "There I saw women working, organizing, teaching themselves. I heard a lot about uplifting the race."[17]

Height battled racism throughout her youth; for example, she applied to

Working at the YWCA

In 1939, Height moved to Washington, D.C., and got a job at the Phyllis

LUCY DIGGS SLOWE

The Lucy Diggs Slowe Hall was named after a black activist who founded many organizations for black women in her time. For example, according to Columbia University, Slowe "was one of the original sixteen founders of Alpha Kappa Alpha Sorority, the first sorority founded by African American women."[1] Sororities are college organizations that help female students connect, make friends, and access leadership opportunities. Due to segregation, these opportunities were lacking for black female college students until Slowe created an organization specifically for them.

Slowe also held leadership positions at several schools. In 1919, she founded the first junior high school in Washington, D.C., and served as its principal until 1922, when she was appointed the College Dean of Women at Howard University—the first black woman to hold that post. Furthermore, as a way to "pool resources, share knowledge, and build collaboration, Slowe founded both the National Association of College Women, which she led for several years as first president, and the Association of Advisors to Women in Colored Schools."[2]

1. "Lucy Diggs Slowe," Columbia University, accessed on May 9, 2019. blackhistory.news.columbia.edu/people/lucy-diggs-slowe.

2. "Lucy Diggs Slowe," Columbia University.

Wheatley Young Women's Christian Association (YWCA). There she worked with young black women who flocked to the nation's capital during World War II to find work. Most of these women were unable to find housing because the city was segregated and had very few living facilities for African Americans. Height documented the problem and presented her findings to the U.S. government. As a result of Height's and others' intervention, the Lucy Diggs Slowe Hall was created specifically for black women to live in while they looked for work in the city.

In 1944, Height moved to New York to become the secretary for interracial education at the YWCA. In this position, she developed guidelines about how to organize and work with interracial groups. She attended the YWCA's national convention in Atlantic City, New Jersey, in 1946 and supported the creation of a document called the Interracial Charter. Among other things, the charter declared, "Wherever there is injustice on the basis of race, whether in the community, the nation, or the world, our protest must be clear and our labor for its removal vigorous and steady."[19]

Despite an outcry by southern delegates who walked out of the convention, the charter was approved, and the organization began to focus its efforts toward racial equality for the first time. The YWCA became one of the first national service organizations to bring black people into leadership positions and to focus on civil rights issues.

President of the NCNW

Height remained active with the YWCA, but that was not her only leadership role. In 1957, she was elected president of the National Council of Negro Women (NCNW), a position she held for the next 40 years. This organization was founded in 1935 by black female activist Mary McLeod Bethune. Under Bethune's leadership, the group worked closely with the NAACP, lobbying for the passage of anti-lynching legislation. The organization also worked on passing laws to end restrictions that prevented black people from voting and obtaining fair housing. In the late 1940s and throughout the next several decades, the group fought for civil rights and for school desegregation. The council also provided leadership and guidance to make black women's voices heard in every area of social and political life.

Height worked right alongside many male leaders of the civil rights movement in roles that were equally as important. In 1960, for instance, Height became the first woman to join the philanthropic Taconic Foundation, a group committed to furthering civil and human rights. Already in the group were Martin Luther King Jr. of the Southern Christian Leadership Conference (SCLC), Whitney Young of the National Urban League, James Farmer of the Congress of Racial Equality, and Roy Wilkins, leader of the NAACP. The Taconic Foundation formed the Council for United Civil Rights Leadership and focused on raising money for civil rights. Altogether, they raised and donated nearly $1 million.

Height and the women of the NCNW also participated in the famous March on Washington on August 28, 1963. The purpose of the march was to protest for jobs and freedom. Two hundred and fifty thousand people from all over the country attended the event.

As the plans were drawn up for the event, several leading women, including Height, approached civil rights activist Bayard Rustin, who was supervising many of the details

FIGHTING FOR VISIBILITY

The March on Washington was not the only time black women were overlooked at a national protest. In 2017, a Women's March was organized, but many black women said they felt as if they had been pushed to the side by the white organizers. Additionally, some black women who attended as protestors remarked that they felt ignored by the white women who were also participating. In a guest article for *HuffPost*, a young black woman named S. T. Holloway gave one example:

> We marched for hours and recited and re-recited every protest chant under the sun … However, in a sea of thousands, at an event billed as a means of advancing the causes affecting all women, the first and last time I heard "Black Lives Matter" chanted was when my two girlfriends and I began to chant. About 40 to 50 others joined in, a comparatively pathetic response to the previous chorus given to the other chants … It represented the continued neglect, dismissal and disregard of the issues affecting black women and other women of color.[1]

In response to this type of protest, the white organizers of the Women's March committed to including more black women in the organization of future events and to promoting a platform of intersectionality, which is "the concept that black women, for example, face a unique kind of discrimination compared to white women because they have multiple identities that are discriminated against. This would also be true of gay women compared to straight women."[2] However, many critics say there is still more such organizations could be doing to give visibility and support to women of color, and black women have continued to prove throughout the years that they will keep fighting to make sure this goal is accomplished.

1. S. T. Holloway, "Why This Black Girl Will Not Be Returning to the Women's March," *HuffPost*, January 19, 2018. www.huffpost.com/entry/why-this-black-girl-will-not-be-returning-to-the-womens-march_n_5a3c1216e4b0b0e5a7a0bd4b.

2. Dan Kopf, "This Is What the Women's March Actually Wants," Quartz, January 19, 2019. qz.com/1528722/the-womens-march-just-released-its-policy-goals/.

of the march, to discuss women's participation. Height suggested to Rustin that it would be appropriate for at least one woman to speak during the program. Rustin and the other leaders of the march, however, decided against having any female U.S. civil rights leaders speak. However, gospel singer Mahalia Jackson gave a performance and Josephine Baker, who renonunced her U.S. citizenship to live in France, spoke to the crowd.

Height and the women of the NCNW were frustrated that so many female leaders had been ignored. Height said, "We could not get women's participation taken seriously ... What actually happened was so disappointing because actually women were an active part of the whole effort. Indeed women were the backbone of the movement."[20] However, Height and the other women realized that they needed to pick their battles and that they would have greater success at achieving their goals if they approached the subject at a later date. She later explained to interviewers, "We accepted [it] because we saw that the whole objective of freedom and equality and jobs and justice was great enough for us to say 'we'll deal with this at another moment' and we did."[21] This display of maturity and levelheadedness from the NCNW helped ensure both that the

March on Washington went smoothly and that Height and her colleagues were later able to advance their own cause. In her autobiography, Height wrote that the failure of the male leadership to allow women to speak helped lead to the acceleration of the women's movement.

Height and the NCNW also played an active role in a 1964 project called Wednesdays in Mississippi (WIM), which was sponsored by the NCNW with help from the YWCA and other women's groups. Hundreds of young people, black and white—some from out of state—participated in this project. Height and the NCNW sent different teams each week to talk with local women in Mississippi. The purpose of these trips was to help women become more aware of their citizenship rights and register to vote. The project's main goals were to establish lines of communication with local women and lend a hand where needed. In addition, its purpose was "to quell [control] violence, ease tensions, and inspire tolerance in racially torn communities. Southern women of goodwill, both black and white, responded positively."[22]

Height was part of the first team that went into Mississippi in the late summer of 1964. While there, Height attended a meeting of Womanpower

Despite the huge role women played in making the March on Washington (shown here) a success, the male leaders of the march did not allow any female civil rights leaders to speak to the crowd.

Unlimited, a group of local black women who were committed to using direct action, including protests and demonstrations, to achieve equality. Wherever the NCNW women went, they were impressed by the dedication of the local women and the young people who were working on voter registration. The WIM teams were asked to return in 1965, and in 1966, the Wednesdays in Mississippi program was renamed and became the NCNW's Workshops in Mississippi.

With the new name came a new goal: fighting poverty. Underlying most of the discussions with local women was the urgent need to provide decent housing for poor black families. The team developed a plan to help the poor own low-cost homes rather than live as renters and presented it to the U.S. Department of Housing and Urban Development (HUD). With help from charitable foundations, houses were built and provided to black families; no down payment was required. The NCNW then organized a Homebuyers

Association, which trained members to manage and maintain their homes through cooperation. Six years after the start of the program, more than 6,000 homes in more than 80 locations had been built as part of the Homeownership Opportunities Program. This experimental public housing program provided the motivation for similar programs across the United States.

For these and other achievements, Height received the Presidential Medal of Freedom from President Bill Clinton in 1994. She also served as an adviser to every president from Dwight Eisenhower to Barack Obama.

Obama, in speaking of Height's life, commented that she had never cared about getting credit and often worked behind the scenes while the movement's male leaders earned more attention and fame. "What she cared about," Obama stated, "was the cause. The cause of justice, the cause of equality, the cause of opportunity, freedom's cause."[23] Today,

Shown here is Dorothy Height receiving the Congressional Gold Medal in 2004. This award is given to citizens who have had a large impact on American history. Along with the Presidential Medal of Freedom, it is the highest award an American civilian can be given.

the NCNW is involved in projects such as helping women in Senegal start their own small businesses and leading campaigns to decrease the obesity rate—an epidemic in the United States among people of all genders and races.

Clubs for Black Women

The National Association of Colored Women's Clubs (NACWC) claims to be the oldest women's organization in the United States. There are chapters all around the country, and the organization's members are "women of color dedicated to uplifting women, children, families, the home and the community through service, community education, scholarship assistance and the promotion of racial harmony among all people,"[24] according to its website.

Black women were inspired to create the NACWC when British activist Florence Balgarnie of the English Anti-Lynching League wrote to James W. Jacks, the president of the Missouri Press Association, in 1895, asking for his help in bringing media attention to the issue of lynching. Jacks responded with a letter insulting all black people—especially women—saying, among other things, that they were born lawbreakers who did not understand the difference between right and wrong. Outraged by this insult, a black woman named Josephine St.

Pierre Ruffin issued a call to action to black women across America. Ruffin had been born into a wealthy family in 1842, so she had advantages that were not available to many other black Americans at the time. She became the first black woman to graduate from Harvard Law School and later achieved a position as a city judge in Boston—again, the first black woman to do so.

Following Ruffin's call to action, a conference was held in 1896 in Washington, D.C., where the attendees agreed to create an organization that would support black women and help them address concerns that were unique to them. For example, many people find jobs through networking, or making social connections. Friends of friends can recommend them for a job or let them know when one will be opening up that they can apply to. However, due to racism and the difficulty many black people have historically had in finding good jobs, there are fewer networking opportunities open to the black community. One of the goals of the NACWC was to help black women make those kinds of connections to help themselves and their children find better opportunities.

Another women's organization was the Phyllis Wheatley Women's Clubs, which was established in 1895. It was named after influential poet Phyllis

The Phyllis Wheatley Women's Clubs got its name from the renowned poet (shown here).

one was established in Nashville, Tennessee, but the organization soon spread northward. According to the website BlackPast,

These northern clubs helped young women who moved from the South to the North, looking for work. It was difficult for African American women to find decent housing and work and the clubs provided services to establish these women in Northern urban society. Some clubs focused on specific objectives. The Buffalo, New York club asked the Buffalo police force to quell vice in the black neighborhoods. It also sought to improve the public library by providing books by African American authors. Like other clubs, however, the Buffalo club raised money to provide a monthly pension for Underground Railroad leader Harriet Tubman.[25]

Wheatley (sometimes spelled Phillis), who was seized from her home in West Africa and sold into slavery in the American South when she was seven years old. After she impressed her owners with her intelligence, they taught her to read and write. Later, they also helped her publish her poetry. She wrote many emotional poems, some of which were comments about slavery, and became famous.

Like the NACWC, the Phyllis Wheatley organization has chapters across the United States. The first

After 1900, some of the clubs remained independent, while others—such as the one Height worked at in Washington, D.C.—merged with the YWCA.

These two black women's organizations have existed for decades, but

Shown here are members of Kimberly Bryant's organization Black Girls Code, which she created to help black girls advance in technology classes.

modern-day women have formed their own organizations to meet modern-day needs. For example, Kimberly Bryant found, when she attended college, that there were very few black women in her computer programming courses. She helped pave the way by getting her degree in electrical engineering and holding leadership positions at several major pharmaceutical and biotech companies, including Merck and Pfizer. Years later, in 2011, she resolved to do something to help young black women excel in science, technology, engineering, and math (STEM) classes, so she created the organization Black Girls Code. This group offers workshops and school courses to introduce programming and coding to black girls when they are young so they will feel more confident pursuing a college degree in these areas when they get older. Organizations such as this one show that black women are still working to raise each other up and help each other excel in all aspects of life.

CHAPTER THREE
LEARNING ABOUT
CITIZENSHIP

Citizenship is not a natural skill. People must be taught what their constitutional rights are, how to register to vote, and how to do research on the candidate they want to support, among other things. For white people, this was not so difficult. They had grown up being taught these things, either directly or indirectly, by their parents, teachers, and other white adults around them. For black people, however, this was much harder. When they were slaves, they were not considered to be citizens, so they never learned these important lessons. Even after slavery ended, they had difficulty learning because white people still wanted black people to remain second-class citizens. Not only did they not want to teach black people how to register to vote, they actively discouraged them from voting with threats or violence. Civil rights leaders such as Septima Clark did the important work of

giving black people citizenship lessons so they could make their voices heard at the polls and stand up for the rights they deserved. Historian Lynne Olson described Septima Clark by saying that she "had a genius for convincing people that they themselves could be leaders, that they did not have to depend on others to show them the way."[26]

A Natural Teacher

Septima Poinsette Clark was born in Charleston, South Carolina, in 1898. She was the second of eight children. She attended Avery Normal Institute, a school founded after the Civil War by the American Missionary Association; it was the only school in Charleston that prepared black people for college.

Though unable to afford any additional education, Clark nonetheless obtained a teaching certificate. She was a natural teacher and loved working with young people, and she used

Voting is an important part of being a citizen, which is why many white people did not want black people to be able to register to vote.

to improve conditions at the poor, mainly black schools she worked at.

While she was teaching at a school in Columbia, South Carolina, Clark also began to work in the kind of citizenship education programs she would later lead. She was asked by Wil Lou Gray, head of the South Carolina adult education program, to help educate illiterate African American soldiers who were stationed at nearby Camp Jackson. This program taught soldiers to sign their names, to read bus routes, and to do basic math.

In 1947, Clark moved back to Charleston to take care of her sick mother. Active in Charleston's black community and well respected in the school system, Clark was always on the lookout for ways to increase her knowledge. In 1954, she decided to attend a workshop at Highlander Folk School at the suggestion of another teacher. The school, which was located in rural Tennessee, brought together people from all over the country to participate in integrated workshops. In these sessions, people learned about community organizing, voter registration, and civil

whatever materials she had to do this. When there were no textbooks, she talked to the students and had them share stories about their homes. When there was no chalkboard, she wrote out these stories on old paper bags; she then used this material in teaching them to read and write. She also began teaching many of her students' parents, most of whom could neither read nor write. Over time, she worked

rights activism. Historian Jacqueline A. Rouse explained, "Advocating equality of the races, Highlander flagrantly [openly] violated segregation laws and customs, and provided integrated housing and other accommodations. Highlander sponsored workshops which concentrated on the elimination of racial stereotypes, the breaking down of social barriers, and the development of leaders."[27]

Clark was excited about what she had learned at Highlander. When she returned to Charleston, she began organizing black teachers, many of whom were having difficulty getting loans to attend graduate programs. White teachers, on the other hand, rarely had any problem qualifying for such loans. With Clark's guidance, the black teachers improved their situation by opening their own credit union that would give them loans.

Fighting to Be Citizens

It was around this time that the landmark decision of *Brown v. Board of Education of Topeka* was handed down by the U.S. Supreme Court. On May 17, 1954, the Court declared that school segregation was unconstitutional. White outrage about this decision led to numerous southern state governments announcing that they would not abide by the court ruling.

South Carolina passed a law stating that no city or state employee could belong to the NAACP. Then the Charleston School Board, in an attempt to determine the loyalty of their employees, also began requiring that all their public school teachers tell the school board what organizations they belonged to outside of work. When Clark listed her membership in the NAACP, she was immediately fired from her teaching job and denied her pension (a payment government employees get after retirement). After 40 years of teaching, Clark found herself unemployed in her mid-50s without any money to support herself.

When the director of Highlander Folk School, Myles Horton, heard that Clark was out of work, he offered her the job of director of workshops at the school. He wanted Clark to focus on providing black people with the necessary literacy skills to become registered voters. To accomplish this, Clark developed what she referred to as the "Two-Eye" theory of education. She used one eye to gather students' views on what they needed to learn and the other eye to picture strategies and teaching methods that would help the students meet their needs.

Clark used people's own experiences to improve their reading and writing skills. For example, students learned

Septima Clark's classes helped many black people take full advantage of their citizenship—for example, by registering to vote, as shown here.

to read the Bible, the newspaper, and road signs, while also learning to write their own names. Clark also spent large amounts of time preparing attendees on the best way to register to vote by coaching them on how to pass the literacy tests. She also wrote several workbooks, such as *Taxes You Must Pay*, to prepare students to become full citizens.

In the meantime, the Highlander Folk School came under fire from the white Tennessee government. State leaders were determined to shut down the school because of its integration policies and citizenship teachings; when legal reasons could not be found, state authorities resorted to other methods. One night in 1959, a group of policemen showed up and burst into the assembly hall. Led by Tennessee attorney general Ab Sloan, the men presented Clark with a warrant to search the premises for liquor. Although they found no alcohol except in one small home on the school grounds, the police arrested Clark and three men and took them to jail in Altamont, Tennessee; Clark was later released on bail. While at the school, the police seized people's personal belongings and destroyed many of the school's important documents.

On August 6, 1959, a preliminary hearing on the liquor charge was held. Some white people who were called as witnesses falsely testified that liquor was routinely served at the school, which would have been illegal because the school did not have a liquor license. The court eventually upheld the charges. On September 16, 1959, the judge ordered the administration building closed, and in February 1960, a circuit court judge revoked the school's charter. The school lost its final appeal in April 1961 and closed its doors. It reopened in the 1980s with a focus on economic issues.

Onward and Upward

Although the closure of the Highlander Folk School was a sad event, it did not stop Clark and others from continuing their mission to promote literacy and citizenship among the black community. When Martin Luther King Jr. and the other leaders of SCLC heard of Clark's success at Highlander, they decided to offer her a similar position with their organization. In 1961, Clark accepted King's invitation to serve as director of education and teaching for SCLC.

Clark's most significant contribution to SCLC became the Voter Education Project, which was created to teach potential voters how to register. She said, "I went to SCLC and worked with Dr. King as director of education and director of teaching. And there traveled from place to place getting people to realize that they wanted to eliminate illiteracy. We had to eliminate illiteracy first! And then after eliminating illiteracy, then we went into registration and voting."[28] Part of Clark's gift, according to historian Taylor Branch, was "recognizing natural leaders among the ... midwives, old farmers ... grandmothers ... and imparting to them her unshakable confidence and respect."[29]

Clark and the other teachers taught by asking questions such as, "What does it mean to be a U.S. citizen?" They used common items such as newspapers and street signs to teach literacy. The students also learned to fill out Social Security forms, money orders, catalog forms, tax returns, and applications for driver's licenses and jobs. In math classes, the students were taught how much money was needed for gas or the length of fencing needed to encircle a field. There were also sessions on black history and classes on nonviolent protest. Many

OVERCOMING BARRIERS TO VOTING

White Southern governments, and sometimes Northern ones as well, took many actions to keep black people from voting. For example, in most southern states, people were required to take a literacy test before they could register to vote; the literacy test, however, was rarely given to white voters. Furthermore, in several documented instances, black people who correctly interpreted a document in English, such as their state's constitution, were then required to read other documents written in foreign languages. The tests were thus created so that black people would fail them.

In addition to the literacy test, many southern states also used the poll tax to restrict black voter registration. Poll taxes, which were taxes that a person had to pay in order to vote, began in the late 19th century as an effort to keep black people—who generally could not afford to pay them—from voting. Intimidation was another voter suppression tactic that was frequently used; white racist groups such as the Ku Klux Klan (KKK) often patrolled areas in the South where black people attempted to register. Violence was common as black people who tried to vote were attacked or threatened.

of these subjects were things white people generally picked up without ever really thinking about it but which black people had never had the opportunity to learn. Clark knew that being poorly educated could make adults feel self-conscious and worry that they might be stupid. By giving them a sense of confidence and encouraging them with lessons they could pick up easily, Clark helped her students overcome their self-doubt and understand that being denied an education does not mean someone is not smart enough to learn.

Citizenship Schools were established in 11 different southern states. To make the classes effective in each region, Clark gathered information about local and state voting requirements, since each state had different laws. Clark explained, "We used the election laws of that particular state to teach the reading. Each state had to have its own particular reading, because each state had different requirements

Black citizens bravely exercised their rights in spite of the threats they received. Shown here is a group taking an oath during a voter registration drive in 1966.

for the election laws."[30] Participants left the workshops with a determination to register to vote and to pass on their new skills to others in their own communities. Branch summarized how effective the study program was by writing, "With drills from basic civics—how to spell 'freedom,' the basic duties of a sheriff—Clark needed only an intensive week's retreat to have most former illiterates proudly signing their names, writing letters, and lining up at the courthouse, able and inspired to register."[31]

For her job, Clark traveled throughout the South recruiting and teaching. Every teacher she trained came from the community in which that person later taught. Writers for the academic journal *Southern Cultures* explained how the schools helped black women in particular. They wrote,

Training sessions and teaching classes afforded grassroots African American women the opportunity to evaluate the local problems they deemed most

important while the Movement itself provided a vehicle for addressing them ...

Graduates put what they had learned into practice by influencing others to register and vote, by assuming leading and supportive roles in local Civil Rights campaigns, and by joining existing organizations or establishing new ones to tackle community welfare needs.[32]

Working Without Support

While the Citizenship Schools led to the registration of hundreds of black voters, the program often lacked the funds it needed to be fully successful. Journalists Mack T. Hines III and Dianne Reed explained,

The Citizenship Schools never received the full support of the SCLC leadership. The reason is that Dr. King and the other SCLC ministerial leaders overlooked Septima Clark's potential to serve as a well-rounded leader of the organization ... Consequently the SCLC leadership failed to consistently provide Septima Clark with the resources needed to

continuously conduct meaningful voter registration workshops.[33]

Despite the lack of support from SCLC, Clark achieved amazing results on her own. She was responsible for providing more than 100 teachers with the training they needed to establish their own Citizenship Schools. She oversaw all the workshops, trained most of the new teachers, and spent time with the participants. She made sure that everyone was treated in a courteous and respectful manner. By 1970, Olson wrote, "some ten thousand citizenship school teachers trained by her and her colleagues had taught more than one hundred thousand blacks to read and write and demand their rights of citizenship."[34] Furthermore, as Clark proudly stated in 1985, "from one end of the South to the other, if you look at black elected officials and the political leaders, you find people who had their first involvement in the training program of the citizenship school."[35]

Clark stayed with SCLC until the early 1970s, when she retired at the age of 72. She eventually returned to Charleston, South Carolina, where she became the first black woman to serve on the Charleston School Board—the same group that had dismissed her for her membership in the NAACP years earlier.

MAKING A DIFFERENCE

The second of four girls whose mother died early, Dorothy Cotton, born in the 1930s, was raised by her abusive father, a laborer in a tobacco factory in Goldsboro, North Carolina. With the help of one of her teachers, she was able to attend Shaw University in Raleigh, North Carolina. She paid for additional expenses by working three jobs while she attended school.

Cotton's life as a civil rights activist began in the late 1950s when she was a graduate student in Petersburg, Virginia. She participated in picketing the local library to protest against segregation. She later moved to Atlanta, Georgia, where she began working for SCLC. Over time, she became the only woman in King's inner circle of aides. She helped organize protests and was injured several times in her work. For example, in 1964, she brought 12 children to a whites-only public beach in St. Augustine, Florida; she and the children waded into the water to protest the segregation policy. Cotton suffered an injury in the ensuing arrest that affected the hearing in her left ear for the rest of her life. However, this did not stop her from continuing her work with SCLC.

Cotton, like Septima Clark, was one of several people involved in the SCLC Citizenship Schools. In her role as teacher and coordinator, she helped train hundreds of black people to vote and participate in political activities. In her classes, she combined singing with other lessons. To help teach reading, for example, she taught the students to sing the words as they spelled them, then held a discussion about what the words meant. In a 2009 interview with NPR, she explained how important the Citizenship Schools were to the black community by saying, "People ... had to unbrainwash themselves, because this sense of being less than other people was hard-wired into the culture."[1] In the late 1980s, Cotton became the director of student activities at Cornell University in Ithaca, New York, where she continued to hold workshops focusing on race relations, women's issues, and nonviolence. She died in 2018 at the age of 88, having dedicated her whole life to fighting racial injustice.

1. Quoted in Richard Sandomir, "Dorothy Cotton, Rights Champion and Close Aide to King, Dies at 88," *New York Times*, June 14, 2018. www.nytimes.com/2018/06/14/obituaries/dorothy-cotton-rights-champion-and-close-aide-to-king-dies-at-88.html.

For six decades, Clark dedicated her life to improving the lives of her fellow black citizens. Historian Karenna Gore Schiff wrote, "Septima was a

Shown here is Septima Clark (center) with Rosa Parks (left) and Parks's mother, Leona McCauley (right).

transformative teacher to thousands of blacks ... who, touched by her influence, became the voters, the marchers, and the organizers of the civil rights movement."[36] One of those women, who went on to become famous, was Rosa Parks.

CHAPTER FOUR
ORGANIZING A LIFE-CHANGING BOYCOTT

A boycott is when people avoid something as a form of protest. A person can engage in a boycott by themselves, but it is far more effective when a lot of people take part. For example, someone who does not like a restaurant's policies may boycott the restaurant by never going to eat there, but this will not affect the restaurant in any way. In contrast, if a boycott against the restaurant is organized and thousands of people stop going there, the restaurant's profits will suffer and it will be more likely to change the policy people object to. This was the principal behind the Montgomery bus boycott—one of the most widely publicized events of the civil rights movement.

Segregation on city buses was the law prior to 1955 in the city of Montgomery, Alabama. Segregation rules required black passengers to sit in the back of the bus; these rules were strictly enforced. If their seats were needed for white passengers, black riders were required to stand. In addition, black people were required to pay for their fares at the front of the bus but then were forced to leave the bus and board through the back door. Often, bus drivers simply drove away before black passengers could enter the bus. To protest such treatment and make a point about overall segregation, black citizens in Montgomery decided to boycott the buses. They stopped riding them for more than a year, sticking to their principles even though they were threatened by whites and often had a difficult time finding other ways to get around town. White people tried everything they could think of to end the boycott because they were aware that if black people pooled their resources, they would be able to enact social change. In the end, this is exactly what happened: The Supreme Court struck down

Under segregation, everything was designed to keep white and black people separate. This photograph shows a segregated bus in Florida, with black passengers in the back and white passengers in the front.

segregation on Montgomery buses in 1956.

Two women played instrumental roles in the Montgomery bus boycott: Jo Ann Robinson and Rosa Parks. While Martin Luther King Jr. received most of the historical credit for the boycott, it was these two women who sparked the protest and then helped organize and carry it out. The boycott was the first successful protest against white domination by significantly large numbers of ordinary black citizens.

Jo Ann and Rosa

Jo Ann Gibson Robinson was born in Culloden, Georgia, the 12th child of a farming family. She became the only one of the twelve children to finish college when she graduated from Georgia State College. After teaching in both California and Texas, Robinson moved to Montgomery, Alabama, in 1949 to teach at the all-black Alabama State College.

It was also in 1949 that Robinson boarded a Montgomery bus to take her to the airport. The bus was nearly

THE CLUB FROM NOWHERE

In the 1960s, it was dangerous for black people to openly protest the way they were treated. Even if they were not targeted for violence, it was common for black activists to be fired from their jobs, which meant they would have difficulty supporting their families. For this reason, some people chose to help the cause in secret. Georgia Gilmore was one such woman, and she provided a way for other women to do the same.

When meetings about the bus boycott and other protests were held by King at the Holt Street Baptist Church in Montgomery, Gilmore sold food she had cooked to those who attended. Gilmore also organized other black women to sell their own food at places such as beauty salons, cab stands (where someone would wait for a taxi), and churches. According to food historian John T. Edge, Gilmore "offered these women, many of whose grandmothers were born into slavery, a way to contribute to the cause that would not raise suspicions of white employers who might fire them from their jobs, or white landowners who might evict them from the houses they rented."[1] The profits of all of these food sales went to pay for transportation—including gas money and repairs for private vehicles—for those who had pledged to boycott the Montgomery buses. Gilmore called her organization the Club from Nowhere because they were raising money secretly, so it officially came from "nowhere."

In February 1956, King and other leaders of the bus boycott were put on trial for unlawful conspiracy, and Gilmore testified on his behalf. This caused her to lose her job at the restaurant where she worked. With King's encouragement, she opened her own business, turning her home into an informal restaurant. She died on March 25, 1990—the 25th anniversary of a nonviolent protest march King led from Selma, Alabama, to Montgomery. NPR reported, "She'd spent the morning preparing chicken and macaroni and cheese to feed people marching in observation of the anniversary. Her family served that food to those who came to mourn her."[2]

1. Quoted in Maria Godoy, "Meet the Fearless Cook Who Secretly Fed—and Funded—the Civil Rights Movement," NPR, January 15, 2018. www.npr.org/sections/thesalt/2018/01/15/577675950/meet-the-fearless-cook-who-secretly-fed-and-funded-the-civil-rights-movement.

2. Godoy, "Meet the Fearless Cook."

empty when she boarded, so she took a seat in the white section. The bus driver immediately began yelling at her to get up from her seat and raised his arm as if to hit her. "I felt ... like a dog,"[37] Robinson later reported.

Partially because of this incident, Robinson became a member of the Women's Political Council (WPC), a group formed by educator Mary Fair Burks in 1946 and made up of professional black women who worked in Montgomery. The group worked on voter registration and sought to make improvements to the black community. Robinson became president of the WPC in the early 1950s.

In May 1954, Robinson, on behalf of the WPC, sent a letter to the mayor of Montgomery about the continued abuse and harassment of black people on the city buses. In the letter, Robinson informed the mayor that the black citizens of Montgomery might boycott the city buses if nothing was done to improve the situation. She pointed out that black people made up about 90 percent of the riders and that the city's downtown stores benefited financially from this high percentage; a boycott could therefore be financially devastating. The mayor and city government ignored the warning, choosing not to improve the situation on the buses.

While city authorities refused to act, a group of people, including Robinson, black attorney Fred Gray, and E.D. Nixon of the NAACP began looking for a person who could serve as a test case to challenge bus segregation in the courts. Eventually, they found their case in Rosa Parks, born Rosa McCauley in Tuskegee, Alabama, in 1913. She attended school at the Montgomery Industrial School for Girls until she was a teenager; at that time, she quit school and got a job as a maid to help support her sick mother. In 1932, she married Raymond Parks, completed her high school education, and attended a few classes at Alabama State College in Montgomery.

Rosa Parks joined the NAACP in 1943. She served as the Montgomery chapter's youth adviser and as the organization's secretary. She called members to remind them of meetings and projects in the black community; answered phones, handled mail, and sent out press releases; and kept track of every complaint that flooded into the office concerning racial violence and discrimination. Parks spent many hours walking through the black community, asking for volunteers and telling people about the kind of work the NAACP was doing.

In addition to working for the NAACP, Parks also held a variety of

While Jo Ann Robinson purposely stayed out of the limelight, Rosa Parks (shown here) became one of the best-known faces of the civil rights movement.

necessary money for Parks to travel to the school.

When Parks returned to Montgomery after her week at Highlander, she found it even harder to endure the bus segregation and other discriminatory laws that were in effect. She had spent the week living on an equal basis with whites, and it was difficult to return to a life where she was surrounded by prejudice and discrimination.

Taking a Stand by Keeping Her Seat

On Thursday, December 1, 1955, Parks boarded a bus in Montgomery, paid the fare, and took a seat in the first row behind the whites-only section. As more and more passengers boarded the bus, the front seats filled quickly, and soon a white passenger was left standing. The driver walked to the back of the bus and ordered Parks and her seatmates to move. There was only one white passenger, but all four black passengers were asked to move since segregation law forbade black people from sitting in any row that a white person was sitting in. The other black passengers did leave their seats, but Parks refused. She

other jobs—everything from being a house cleaner to a seamstress. One of her best customers was a white woman named Virginia Durr, a well-known civil rights activist in the Montgomery area. In the spring of 1955, Durr got a phone call from Highlander Folk School leader Myles Horton asking if she knew anyone who could benefit from a scholarship to the school. Durr immediately thought of Parks and raised the

CLAUDETTE COLVIN

Although Rosa Parks is often credited with being the first black woman to refuse to give up her seat on a Montgomery bus, it was actually 15-year-old Claudette Colvin who laid the groundwork for the Montgomery bus boycott. Like Parks, Colvin refused to give up her seat for a white passenger when the bus driver told her to; she said, "It's my constitutional right to sit here as much as that lady. I paid my fare, it's my constitutional right."[1] She was arrested but released later that night after her minister paid her bail.

The NAACP briefly considered using Colvin as their champion, but ultimately went with Parks because Colvin was so young and because she was a single teenage mother, which the group felt might be used against her in court to distract from the issue of segregation. However, Colvin herself claimed in an interview with NPR that she was passed over because the NAACP "thought I would be too militant for them. They wanted someone mild and genteel like Rosa."[2] Colvin did end up going to court with three other plaintiffs in the case *Browder v. Gayle*, which found bus segregation unconstitutional in 1956.

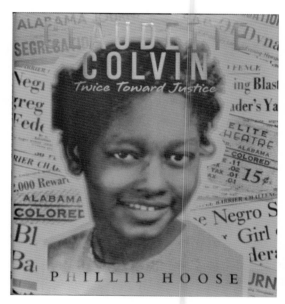

Shown here is a young Claudette Colvin on the cover of a book about her life.

1. Quoted in "Claudette Colvin," Biography.com, last updated April 12, 2019. www.biography.com/activist/claudette-colvin.

2. Quoted in Alicia Lutes, "Claudette Colvin: Meet the Teenager Who Inspired Rosa Parks," Amy Poehler's Smart Girls, May 19, 2015. amysmartgirls.com/claudette-colvin-meet-the-teenager-who-inspired-rosa-parks-f96d2335ebbc.

later explained, "I had been pushed as far as I could stand to be pushed. I had decided that I would know once and for all what rights I had as a human being and a citizen ... People always say that I didn't give up my seat because I was tired, but that isn't true. I was not tired physically ... No, the only tired I was, was tired of giving in."[38]

Parks was later accused of acting on behalf of the NAACP, but that was not the case. Journalist David Halberstam explained, "Later the stunned white leaders of Montgomery repeatedly charged that Parks's refusal was part of a carefully orchestrated plan on the part of the local NAACP, of which she was an officer. But that was not true; what she did represented one person's exhaustion with a system that dehumanized all black people."[39]

Parks insisted that she had no intention of getting arrested when she boarded the bus. Years afterward, she reflected on her thoughts that day. "When I got on the bus that evening I wasn't thinking about causing a revolution or anything of the kind," she said. "I was thinking about my husband ... I was thinking about my back aching ... I told myself I wouldn't put up no fuss against them arresting me ... But I also knew I wasn't gonna give up my seat just because a white driver told me to; I'd already done that too many times."[40]

It was only later that Parks realized that her isolated act had helped spark the civil rights movement and the kind of protest that proved most productive. She had shown that the actions of individual citizens were important. In the late 1950s and all through the 1960s, individuals would again and again take action, small and large, in their own efforts to stand up against the forces of segregation.

Parks was released on bail, and that night, she and her husband met with Nixon and Gray to discuss her upcoming trial. Nixon asked her if she would be a test case so the NAACP could challenge bus segregation. Rosa was torn; she knew this course of action could be dangerous and she did not want to put her family at risk, but she also was fed up with the indignities she and other black riders faced on the buses. She finally stated, "If you think it will mean something to Montgomery and do some good, I'll be happy to go along with it."[41]

Getting Organized

That same evening, after meeting with Rosa Parks, Nixon and Gray contacted Jo Ann Robinson about the possibility of boycotting the buses on Monday, December 5—the day of Parks's trial. Robinson immediately put the plans for such a boycott into effect; she and the women of the WPC had, in fact, already started planning for such an event. They stayed up all night, using equipment at the Alabama State University campus to make more than 35,000 copies of a flier they could hand out. The women who created this flier did so with great stealth; if the white authorities who controlled the university found out what they were doing, they would have been fired from their teaching positions.

The flier that Robinson created read:

Another Negro woman has been arrested and thrown into jail because she refused to get up out of her seat on the bus and give it to a white person ... Negroes have rights, too ... If we do not do something to stop these arrests, they will continue. The next time it may be you, or your daughter, or mother. The woman's case will come up on Monday. We are, therefore, asking every Negro to stay off the buses Monday in protest of the arrest and trial. Don't ride the buses to work, to town, to school, or anywhere on Monday.[42]

Hundreds of women worked through the night distributing the flier to dozens of locations, including beauty shops, barbershops, factories, churches, and storefronts. The word spread quickly. By the end of the weekend, nearly every black person in the city of Montgomery knew about the plans for the boycott.

The black citizens of Montgomery eagerly waited for Monday morning. Robinson later described it, saying,

Monday morning ... I shall never forget because many of us had not gone to bed that night ... We had been up waiting for the first buses to pass to see if any riders were on them. It was a cold morning, cloudy, there was a threat of rain, and we were afraid that if it rained the people would get on the bus. But as the buses began to roll, and there were one or two on some of the buses, none on some of them, then we began to realize that the people were cooperating ... As a result, a very negligible number of riders rode that first day.[43]

In fact, more than 50,000 black people chose not to ride the buses that day. Meanwhile, Parks had her day in court. She had been told by her lawyers that she was not to testify. The NAACP wanted her to be found guilty so they could appeal the conviction to a higher court, where the segregation

Shown here is a depiction of the Montgomery bus boycott at the National Civil Rights Museum. The exhibit shows several black people continuing to walk down the street, ignoring the bus that has pulled up beside them.

laws could be changed. She was found guilty on December 5, 1955, of violating the city's segregation laws and ordered to pay a fine of $10 plus $4 for court costs—a large sum of money at the time, especially for a poor black woman. Her attorneys immediately filed an appeal, which would eventually be heard by the U.S. Supreme Court.

That same night, hundreds of black people showed up at a mass meeting at Holt Street Baptist Church. The meeting had been called to discuss the future of the boycott. As a result of Parks's arrest and the meeting at the church, a new organization was created—the Montgomery Improvement Association (MIA), under the leadership of Martin Luther King Jr. The group pledged to continue the boycott until bus segregation was ended in the city.

Before Parks's arrest and the meeting, King and many other black ministers in Montgomery had been reluctant to speak out against or fight segregation. Now they realized that if they did not respond to the mass outpouring of people supporting the boycott, they would lose their credibility with their congregations. King, when he accepted the leadership of the MIA, stated he would support the boycott but did not want to organize it. Fortunately, Robinson already had that covered.

The boycott was, in fact, organized and led by Robinson and other women. One such person was Irene West, a wealthy black resident of Montgomery. West, despite being close to 80 years old, drove through the city every morning during the boycott, picking up people who needed a ride. Hundreds of white women also helped the boycott succeed by picking up their maids and other employees. Giving these black employees rides to work meant they did not have to make the difficult choice between supporting the boycott and supporting their families by keeping their jobs.

As the boycott continued, all 18 black cab companies agreed to pick up black passengers for low fares. When the police started arresting black cab drivers for not charging full price, the MIA asked for volunteer drivers. Robinson drove one car, while Parks served as the dispatcher for the other drivers, telling them where to go to pick up people who needed a ride. Service was provided from 5:30 in the morning until 12:30 at night; in all, 30,000 black people were transported each day to and from work. White and black drivers alike were harassed by the police, who handed out hundreds of tickets every day, even though the drivers were not violating any traffic laws.

Despite the harassment, the black citizens of Montgomery stayed off the buses for 381 days. The U.S. Supreme Court finally ruled on the case on November 13, 1956. The court upheld a federal district court ruling of June 4, 1956, that had stated that Alabama's segregation laws for buses were unconstitutional, since citizens were being denied their equal rights. This led to a city law that allowed black people to sit wherever they liked on buses. On December 21, black people returned to the buses victorious.

King later praised Robinson for her efforts, saying, "Apparently indefatigable [untiring], she, perhaps, more than any other person, was active on every level of the protest. She took part in both the executive board and the strategy committee meetings. When the Montgomery Improvement Association newsletter was inaugurated a few months after the protest began, she became its editor."[44] Burks, founder of the WPC, also gave credit to Robinson:

Once [the boycott] was under-
way, nobody worked more

diligently than she did as a representative of the board of the MIA and as a representative of the WPC. Although others had contemplated a boycott, it was due in large part to Jo Ann's unswerving belief that it could be accomplished, and her never-failing optimism that it would be accomplished, and her selflessness and unbounded energy that it was accomplished.[45]

Robinson continued her teaching career after the successful boycott. She taught at Alabama State University in the 1960s, then briefly at Grambling College in Louisiana. She eventually moved to Los Angeles, California, where she worked as a teacher until the late 1970s. Thelma Glass, a former member of the WPC, praised Robinson by saying, "In all my years working and living with civic and educational activities, I have never met a woman who was more courageous than Jo Ann Robinson."[46]

Continuing to Work Toward Equality

Both Rosa and Raymond Parks lost their jobs because of the boycott. Unable to find work and not feeling safe in Montgomery, the couple eventually moved to Detroit, Michigan, where Rosa ended up working for 20 years as the receptionist in the Michigan office of U.S. House representative John Conyers. The couple also founded the Rosa and Raymond Parks Institute for Self-Development in 1987, a career counseling center for black youth. Rosa was awarded the Presidential Medal of Freedom, one of the highest honors for civilians in the United States, in 1996. Upon her death in 2005, Parks became the first woman to lie in honor in the U.S. Capitol rotunda, and in 2013, she became the first black woman to be honored with a statue in the National Statuary Hall in Washington, D.C. At the statue's unveiling, President Barack Obama talked about how Parks's courage continues to be an inspiration. *USA Today* reported, "All too often, faced with children who are hungry, neighborhoods 'ravaged by violence' and families hobbled by unemployment or illness ... too many people simply throw up their hands and say there's nothing they can do. 'Rosa Parks tells us there's always something we can do,' Obama said."[47]

CHAPTER FIVE
DESEGREGATING SCHOOLS

The Supreme Court upheld segregation in all areas of society as long as the accommodations available for people of color were equal to those available for white people. In practice, this was almost never the case, but it was especially noticeable and had negative long-term effects in schools. The buildings were frequently in disrepair; the learning materials were substandard—for example, textbooks were outdated or falling apart—if they were even available at all; and there was little to no funding for things such as after-school activities or school lunch programs. Such poor learning conditions made it difficult for black students to achieve good grades, which had a huge impact on their ability to get good jobs in the future. This made school desegregation, or integration, a major focus for civil rights groups.

In the early 1950s, the NAACP found several test cases that could challenge the "separate but equal" decision of the Court. These cases led to the landmark ruling in *Brown v. Board of Education*. The Court handed down its decision on May 17, 1954, stating that segregated schools were unconstitutional because such schools were not equal. The Court ordered the southern states to begin the process of integrating their schools.

Desegregation came slowly in the South. Arkansas had integrated a few of its schools in various locations, but little had been done in the state's capital, Little Rock. Arkansas NAACP president and civil rights activist Daisy Bates took it upon herself to lead the effort to desegregate Central High School in that city. She quickly became the adviser to the nine black students—a group that came to be called the Little Rock Nine—who were chosen to integrate the school. Her house was the official pickup and drop-off site for the students; it was also where the press gathered

Ruby Bridges (shown here being protected by federal marshals) became famous as the first black child to integrate an elementary school in the segregated South. As an adult, she continued to work for equality, and in 1999, she created the Ruby Bridges Foundation to promote this goal.

Already an Activist

Daisy Lee Gatson was born in Huttig, Arkansas, in 1914. While she was a baby, her mother was raped and killed by white men. Fearing for his life, her father ran away. Daisy was adopted and raised by Orlee and Susie Smith, friends of her family. Daisy did not find out about the murder of her mother until she was eight. Because the perpetrators had never been punished, Daisy nursed a hatred of whites for most of her life. Eventually, she would turn this hatred toward working to end the humiliation and discrimination that she and other black people faced every day.

Daisy's activism started long before her involvement in the Court-ordered integration. In 1941, her husband, L.C. Bates, started a newspaper called the *Arkansas State Press*. The paper offered local and national news to the black community, with an emphasis on civil rights. Daisy Bates soon began writing articles and editorials for the paper that were highly critical of segregation.

each day. Throughout the long ordeal, Bates was the students' counselor and protector. One of the students, Ernest Green, later described Bates by saying, "She was a quarterback, the coach. We were the players."[48] Historians credit Bates's persistence in integrating Little Rock's Central High School with bringing the school desegregation issue to the forefront of public awareness.

Bates got a lot of backlash for her articles from whites, especially for one she wrote about an incident of police brutality in which a black man had been shot five times while lying on the ground. She had witnessed the incident and also interviewed others who had been present. Her article focused on the prejudice and discrimination that had led to the shooting, which the police claimed was justified.

Highly critical of what had occurred, Bates and her husband called on the black leaders of Little Rock to perform their own investigation; the Negro Citizens' Committee was formed and ruled that the police had acted unprofessionally. The committee sent its report to several authorities, including President Franklin Roosevelt. Federal authorities eventually agreed that the shooting had not been justified. Charges were later filed against one of the policemen, but a white grand jury in Little Rock dismissed the charges; no one was ever punished for the crime.

Opposing Segregation in the Face of Threats

By the early 1950s, Little Rock government officials were beginning to make a few small changes regarding segregation. The Little Rock Zoo, for instance, began admitting black visitors, and a few downtown hotels were allowing organizations with black members to use their meeting rooms. Despite this relaxation of the segregation law, Daisy Bates felt that the government was not doing enough. She ran for and was elected president of the Arkansas NAACP in 1952. Due to low membership numbers, however, the organization was unable to accomplish anything of significance during the first few years of her presidency.

After *Brown v. Board of Education*, some states began integrating their public schools fairly quickly, but since the Court had not given a deadline for full integration, many state governments took no action. Bates learned in a meeting with Arkansas lawmakers in 1954 that the city of Little Rock would integrate slowly. Not satisfied with a plan to start with high school students in 1957 and gradually incorporate other grades over the next three years, Bates took action.

Disgusted with the slowness of the plan, Bates met with national NAACP leaders in late 1955. With their assistance, she helped organize 33 black students, from first grade to high school. All of the students applied to white schools; all were denied admission. Eventually, Bates and the NAACP filed a lawsuit in federal court charging the schools with discrimination. The federal judge, however, ruled that the Little

INTEGRATION STRUGGLES ON COLLEGE CAMPUSES

In February 1956, 26-year-old black student Autherine Lucy was admitted to the University of Alabama, but a mob of whites prevented her from entering the administration building by throwing eggs and other objects at her. Not to be discouraged, Lucy went to classes escorted by the police. The stress on the young college student, however, was immense, and her health began to decline. She was suspended from the university in her first semester, supposedly for her own protection. She was then reinstated, then expelled, and once again reinstated. Finally, she had had enough; she withdrew from the school. Lucy was finally granted her degree from the University of Alabama in 1992.

Charlayne Hunter-Gault had a similar experience at the University of Georgia in 1961. She explained, "On January 9, 1961, I walked onto the campus at the University of Georgia to begin registering for classes ... The officials at the university had been fighting for a year and a half to keep me out. I was not socially, intellectually, or morally undesirable. I was Black. And no Black student had ever been admitted to the University ... in its 176-year history."[1] Hunter-Gault was 19 at the time and suffered extreme bullying and threats of violence during her time at school. Despite these obstacles, she graduated two years later, becoming one of the first two black people ever to graduate from the University of Georgia.

1. Quoted in Bettye Collier-Thomas and V.P. Franklin, eds., *Sisters in the Struggle: African American Women in the Civil Rights–Black Power Movement*. New York, NY: New York University Press, 2001, p. 75.

Rock Board of Education was not violating the law because it was moving at a reasonable speed toward integration. Other appeals were likewise denied.

The admission of black students to all-white Central High School in Little Rock was scheduled to take place on September 3, 1957. During the summer before the school year, Superintendent of Schools Virgil T. Blossom chose nine black students to enter the all-white high school. The Little Rock Nine included Minnijean Brown, Elizabeth Eckford, Ernest Green, Thelma Mothershed, Melba Pattillo, Gloria Ray, Terrence Roberts, Jefferson

Thomas, and Carlotta Walls.

Bates immediately began to meet with the group and give them advice, telling them that they could expect to encounter anger and probably violence from white students and others. Pattillo later wrote about her first meeting with Bates, "She seemed very calm and brave considering the caravans of segregationists said to be driving past her house and tossing firebombs and rocks through her windows. They saw her as their enemy."[49]

During this entire period, Bates had been under constant verbal and sometimes physical attack. In one of the earliest attacks, a rock was thrown through her window. Bates wrote about the incident in her autobiography: "I threw myself to the floor. I was covered with shattered glass ... I reached for the rock lying in the middle of the floor. There was a note tied to it ... Scrawled in bold print were the words: STONE THIS TIME. DYNAMITE NEXT."[50] She was also arrested on numerous occasions on false charges.

During the middle of the school crisis, many of her critics had warned Bates that if she continued to fight for integration, they would destroy her ability to earn a living, and they followed through with this threat. White segregationists applied pressure to those who advertised in the *Arkansas State Press*, resulting

Daisy Bates (standing) became a mentor to the Little Rock Nine.

Bates is shown here standing in her window, which she repaired and taped to prevent it from shattering into small pieces if another vandal tried to break it.

in a significant loss in circulation. Hundreds of white readers canceled their subscriptions; many black readers also canceled because they feared violence would be aimed at them as well if they did not. By 1959, the paper had ceased publication.

Following Through

A number of last-minute attempts were made by Arkansas citizens and authorities to prevent the students' admission. On August 27, 1957, for instance, an injunction—a court order that prevents another court order from being carried out—against integrating the school was filed by the Mothers' League, a group committed to maintaining segregation. Governor Orval E. Faubus appeared as a witness and supported the injunction, warning the court of potential race riots and violence if the black students were admitted. The judge ruled in favor of the Mothers' League. Three days later, the NAACP asked the U.S. District Court to overrule the injunction. This was granted; the judge warned that no one should interfere with the students. In response, Faubus mobilized the Arkansas National Guard on

STUDENTS DEMANDING CHANGE

In 1951, Barbara Johns was a junior at Robert R. Moton High School, a black school in Farmville, Virginia. She and her classmates were frustrated with the horrible conditions of the school they attended. Many classes were held in shacks or old buses, and the all-white school board did not allow the school's students to take courses such as geometry, algebra, world history, or geography.

Johns and a few of her friends decided to see if they could improve the conditions at their school. On the morning of April 23, 1951, they got the principal out of the school by making a false telephone call about students skipping school. Once that had been accomplished, Johns passed the word that there was a meeting in the assembly hall. Johns then took the stage, asked the teachers to leave, and told the students they needed to go on strike for better school accommodations. The students agreed; they refused to attend classes and surrounded the school carrying signs demanding better conditions.

When the school superintendent refused to meet their demands, Johns met with a representative of the NAACP named Oliver Hill. Hill and his partners agreed to take the students' case if their parents were willing to fight not only for a new school but for desegregation of the school district. The parents agreed, and the strike ended after two weeks. The case later became known as *Davis v. County School Board of Prince Edward County*. The NAACP eventually combined this case with several others, resulting in the *Brown v. Board of Education* case that went to the Supreme Court.

September 2 and ordered guardsmen to surround the high school. That night, Faubus gave a televised speech in which he warned, "Blood will run in the streets if Negro students should attempt to enter Central High School."[51]

The next morning, the National Guard refused to allow the students to enter the building. Journalist David Halberstam described the scene:

As they [the students] approached the school, they were ... threatened [by a white mob]; when they finally reached the school, they were turned away by a National

Guard captain, who said he was acting under the orders of Governor Faubus ... The confidence of the mob grew greater by the minute as it found that law enforcement officials were on its side ... Sensing this the ministers and children quickly retreated.[52]

Nearly three weeks passed before another attempt was made to integrate the school. Bates continued to meet with the students, offering support and encouragement. During that time, President Dwight Eisenhower was in frequent contact with Governor Faubus. The president was furious that Faubus had defied the Supreme Court and had disobeyed the judge who had ordered that integration should proceed. After a meeting of the two men and another hearing, Faubus, realizing that he might be arrested, decided to remove the troops. The students would try again to enter the high school on Monday, September 23.

The nine students met at Bates's house that Monday morning. Bates gave the students an encouraging speech, reminding them "again and again that they were doing this not for themselves but for others, some as yet unborn. They were now, like it or not, leaders in a moral struggle."[53]

Bates was in contact with the Little Rock Police, who promised to escort the students into the school. The police kept their promise and snuck the students in a side door while a large white crowd gathered outside. When the crowd learned that the students were already inside the school, violence broke out. The police force was not enough to control the riot, so the students were sent home for their own safety. They were escorted out a back entrance by the police and driven home.

Because Bates had kept the press informed, the event made the front pages of newspapers across the country. This led to outcries from concerned citizens, who begged the president to act. The students stayed home the next day and watched Eisenhower announce on television that night that he was sending in federal troops. More than 1,200 soldiers from the 101st Airborne Division arrived and took up positions around the high school. Bates was notified that the students could safely return to the school.

The next morning, the students met at Bates's house and were driven to school by the soldiers. Surrounding the group of students were 22 soldiers, and surrounding the school itself were 350 paratroopers. An army helicopter flew overhead to keep an eye out for trouble. Each of the nine young people

Shown here is Elizabeth Eckford, one of the Little Rock Nine, walking calmly into school past a mob of anti-integration whites.

take the problem to the National Guard. She spoke to the commander of the troops, as well as city and state government officials, but nothing was done. Bates continued not only to write about the problems the students were having but also to speak out about them publicly. Finally, a guardsman was assigned to each student, although this did not discourage many of the white students from continuing their harassment and abuse of the black group. After a stressful and violent year, however, the one senior among the nine students, Ernest Green, graduated from Central High School in the spring of 1958. He was the first black person to do so.

was given a personal escort who stayed with the student throughout the day.

By the first of October, the situation had calmed enough that the federal troops were withdrawn. The Arkansas National Guard was supposed to take their place, but even with federal orders to protect the children, the National Guard refused to do so. Bates kept careful records of each time the black students were bullied or threatened, and in November, she took the material to Blossom. Blossom thought Bates was exaggerating and advised her to

School Segregation Today

During the summer of 1958, the national press frequently praised Bates and the Little Rock Nine. They dined with the governor of New York and were also given a private tour of the White House. On July 11, 1958,

THE RIGHT QUALITIES

Brown v. Board of Education was the lawsuit that succeeded in integrating schools, so it is the most famous. However, numerous similar lawsuits failed before 1954. Interestingly, nearly all of the plaintiffs in those cases were young girls, and after integration, most of the students chosen to be the pioneers of desegregation were also girls. Rachel Devlin, associate professor of history at Rutgers University and author of *A Girl Stands at the Door*, a book about the black girls who laid the groundwork for integration, explained why girls were at the forefront of this movement:

> *These choices were made on a level that was not always conscious. Parents would explain why they should file a lawsuit, and girls agreed. Many of them said, "I was willing" ... The other thing about girls is that they were good at it. To speak to principals and lawyers and the press you have to be poised, you have to be personable and diplomatic, and young black women had these attributes. They dealt with constant verbal and sexual harassment on the streets ... and they were acutely aware of their self-presentation in public. It was drilled into them as a way to protect their dignity. Also, very few African American girls and young women did not at some point in their lives work in a white home, and they had to learn how to navigate around white people.*

> *But I want to be clear. This was not just about being accommodating—they knew how to stand their ground. Girls were good at combining different forms of bravery; they could be both stubborn and tough, but also project social openness. They had that sense of self-possession that was extremely useful in these situations.*[1]

1. Quoted in Melinda D. Anderson, "The Forgotten Girls Who Led the School-Desegregation Movement," *The Atlantic*, May 30, 2018. www.theatlantic.com/education/archive/2018/05/rachel-devlin-school-desegregation/561284/.

Bates and the students were given the NAACP's highest honor, the Spingarn Medal. However, in spite of all of this, integration came slowly to Little Rock; by 1962, only 80 black students were attending white schools.

Bates continued her work for the NAACP and SCLC. In the 1960s, President John F. Kennedy appointed her to the Democratic National Committee; she also served as an adviser to President Lyndon B. Johnson on his antipoverty campaign. After her husband's death in 1980, she revived the newspaper they had worked on together. She again focused on civil rights issues and kept the paper going until 1987.

Through the hard work and courage of people such as Daisy Bates and the Little Rock Nine, schools across the country were eventually successfully integrated. However, while it is no longer illegal for black students to attend school with white students, systemic segregation remains in effect. "Systemic" means that something is a cultural practice but is not upheld by any specific law.

In 2016, *U.S. News & World Report* published an article about the current state of segregation in American schools. The article's author, Lauren Camera, wrote that according to a report from the Government Accountability Office, "from school year 2000–2001 to 2013–2014, the percentage of K–12 public schools that were high poverty and comprised [made up] of mostly black or Hispanic students grew ... from 9 percent to 16 percent. And the number of students attending those schools more than doubled, from 4.1 million to 8.4 million."[54] Schools that are mainly attended by students of color are disproportionately poor; that 16 percent of schools represents 61 percent of all high-poverty schools. As in the time of legal segregation, this has serious consequences for the students' learning environment. Aside from the fact that a school with more money can afford better books, benefits, and opportunities for its students, a school with a diverse student body offers better social benefits in multiple areas. Genevieve Siegel-Hawley, assistant professor at Virginia Commonwealth University School of Education, explained, "When kids are exposed to children who are different than them, whether it's along racial lines or economic lines, that contact between different groups reduces the willingness of kids to make stereotypes and generalizations about other groups."[55] Research has also shown that truly desegregated schools, where no one racial group is in the majority, "are linked to important benefits, like prejudice reduction, heightened civic engagement and analytical thinking, and better learning outcomes in general."[56]

Part of the reason for this rising school segregation is that families of color are disproportionately poor and live in undesirable school districts. Some areas have proposed rezoning the school districts to make it easier for students of color to attend the wealthier schools, but this has received pushback from wealthy white families who worry that their school district will change as well and their children will end up attending one of the poorer schools. Busing programs ran from about 1971 to 2002 to take students from mostly black neighborhoods to their integrated schools, as many poor families had no car and the schools were often too far away for students to walk to. With the end of the busing programs, it became harder for students of color to get to the better schools. Furthermore, a 1991 Supreme Court case called *Board of Education v. Dowell* ruled that desegregation plans were never meant to be permanent, so schools were no longer monitored to make sure they were truly integrated. Even in schools that are integrated, students of color are often discouraged from taking more challenging classes, causing individual classes to be segregated.

Although school desegregation is still an uphill battle decades after Daisy Bates forced Little Rock to obey the Supreme Court's orders, there is hope for the future, and black women are once again at the forefront of the fight. In 1970, Rita Jones Turner became one of the first black students to attend Vestavia Hills High School in Birmingham, Alabama, after forced desegregation. She remembered that often the school bus would not stop on her street; when it did and she arrived at school, she was placed into remedial classes even though she did not need extra help. At lunchtime, white students harassed her by tearing barrettes from her hair.

Thirty-six years later, Jones Turner received a note from her old school informing her of its attempt to change the policy of desegregation and force her ninth-grade son to enroll elsewhere. Specifically, the school district filed a court motion to stop forced integration. Jones Turner's own experience at Vestavia Hills remained a painful memory, but she resented any attempts at turning back the clock on progress. "We were used, mistreated, downtrodden, and discriminated against," said Jones Turner. "I have no problem with being a sacrificial lamb for the good of the community, but to have the system back out now is not fair. They made a commitment to educate black children."[57]

CHAPTER SIX

STUDENT PROTESTS

Students are often at the forefront of social change, and the civil rights movement was no exception. The Student Nonviolent Coordinating Committee (SNCC) was established in 1960 by students who had been involved in the lunch counter sit-ins in the South. Hundreds of students, black and white, had challenged segregation at all-white lunch counters and had succeeded in integrating many of the restaurants. When King asked SNCC to merge with SCLC, activist leader Ella Baker encouraged the students of SNCC to remain an independent organization. In part because of Baker's advice, SNCC went on to play a major role in voter registration and civil rights protests throughout the South in the years that followed.

In addition to SNCC, Baker was involved in more than 30 different organizations and civil rights campaigns throughout her life. Through her various grassroots efforts, she nurtured a generation of activists to carry forward the civil rights movement. Her leadership often went unnoticed, but taken together, her contributions had an undeniable and lasting impact, even to the present day. The website of the Ella Baker Center for Human Rights states, "Like her, we spark change by unlocking the power of every person to strengthen their communities and shape their future."[58]

Seeing the Struggle Firsthand

Ella Josephine Baker was born in Norfolk, Virginia, in 1903 and grew up in Littleton, North Carolina. There she witnessed a lot of intelligent and determined black people working toward building a strong community. Her parents stressed the importance of economic self-sufficiency and racial pride—two values that played a large

Students played a crucial role in the battle for civil rights, proving that young people have just as much power as adults. This photo of SNCC members was taken in 1964.

role in shaping Baker's worldview as she grew up.

After graduating from Shaw University in Raleigh, North Carolina, in 1927, Baker moved to New York City. One of the few occupations available to educated black women at the time was teaching. However, Baker turned down teaching jobs, preferring instead to work several low-paying jobs in various civil rights organizations.

Living in an area of New York City known as Harlem, Baker was astounded by the poverty and hunger she saw in the black community there. She saw people living in falling-down shacks without running water or basic sanitation. Hundreds of people went hungry because they did not have the money to buy even the most basic kinds of food. Baker participated in various civil rights campaigns; she protested the unfair treatment of black domestic workers, for instance, and helped launch the Young Negroes Cooperative League, a group whose actions were dedicated to improving the economic strength of the black community in Harlem. These workers were employed by some of the richest people in the New York area yet were paid very little and had to endure long hours and backbreaking work. She also began working for a government program that helped promote literacy among the poor workers of New York City.

During the 1930s, Baker worked for the Workers' Education Project of the

For much of its history, Harlem has been a predominately black neighborhood.
Shown here is the 420 block of Lenox Avenue, Harlem, as it appeared in 1938.

Works Progress Administration (WPA) of the federal government. The WPA employed millions of unskilled workers to build roads and other projects, helped feed children, and distributed food and clothing during the Great Depression. The Workers' Education Project focused on literacy and providing educational opportunities for all citizens. Baker offered courses and workshops throughout the Harlem area aimed at educating black people so they could find better-paying jobs. She was also associated with the Harlem branch of the YWCA and met its leader, Dorothy Height. Height and other female friends helped mold Baker into the passionate activist she was already becoming.

Working for the NAACP

Because of the experience Baker had obtained in Harlem and elsewhere, she was offered a position in the NAACP in 1940, first as a field secretary and later as its national director. She was the perfect person for the job because one of her greatest gifts was her ability to organize people. During her years as field secretary for the NAACP, she traveled throughout the South, organizing youth chapters everywhere she went. Never condescending, she treated young people as intelligent individuals who had much to offer the NAACP.

Baker also spoke to local NAACP chapters in the towns she visited and helped those groups increase their membership. She encouraged these local groups to focus on segregation problems in their local area. She made contact with many people during her travels and often stayed in their homes as she moved from place to place. Through these contacts, Baker earned the trust of hundreds of people. Historians Bettye Collier-Thomas and V.P. Franklin stated, "Her travels throughout the South in the 1940s as field secretary for the NAACP provided her with the personal knowledge needed for organizing the black working class."[59] During that period, Baker met and talked with thousands of ordinary black citizens of all ages and genders. Unlike other organizers, who tended to talk down to rural Southerners, she treated everyone with respect. As a result, she formed friendships wherever she went and learned what these individuals wanted in terms of civil rights and equality. These relationships later provided her with a core group of people who could form a mass movement.

Baker eventually became the NAACP's national director, making her the highest-ranking female officer in the organization. It was her task to supervise field secretaries and coordinate local group activities with the goals of the national organization. She helped individual branch offices launch local campaigns in protest against segregation and encouraged the local offices to report any court case that might interest the NAACP legal team.

The NAACP's reliance on legal tactics such as lawsuits to fight discrimination, however, frustrated Baker, who preferred more direct action, such as marches and protests. She also became dissatisfied with the NAACP's focus on increasing membership rather than addressing local issues, such as police brutality or school segregation. She wanted the organization to help empower people to take action on their own behalf. In 1946, she quit her job, although she did continue to work with the New York branch of the NAACP.

In Friendship

After leaving the NAACP, Baker cofounded In Friendship, an organization in the New York area that offered

GLORIA RICHARDSON

Gloria Richardson grew up in Cambridge, Maryland. Although voting had been legal for black people there since the 19th century, obvious racism in Cambridge prevented true equality and kept most black people from exercising this right. Black people also still suffered discrimination in education, jobs, housing, and medical care. The majority of black people in the city were poor and unemployed; those who had jobs worked in very poor conditions. Richardson came from a family that was wealthier than most, but her family's money did not protect them from discrimination. For example, although her uncle and father could afford to go to a hospital when they got sick, both were turned away because they were black, leading to their deaths.

In 1962, Richardson, a graduate of Howard University, helped organize the Cambridge Nonviolent Action Committee, a group dedicated to improving the economic situation of the black community through desegregation of jobs, schools, and housing. The city refused to work with the committee, so the protestors organized several nonviolent protests, such as rallies and sit-ins. However, when white police beat a group of protesting black teens in the summer of 1963, the protestors responded with force. In contrast to King, who advocated a peaceful approach no matter what happened, Richardson believed that "if they come to where you live then defend yourself. I always believed if they came and attacked you you had a right to respond."[1]

The fighting in Cambridge lasted for weeks. The city erupted in shootings, arson, and bomb threats. Within a few days, the minority sections of the city were sealed off with roadblocks manned by Maryland state troopers. Martial law and an 8 p.m. curfew were imposed. The National Guard was called in to keep order. A committee was finally convened in the nation's capital that included, among others, Richardson, Attorney General Robert Kennedy, and

financial support for black people who were actively fighting for civil rights. The group was dedicated to helping those who were suffering economic retaliation because of their fight against segregation. Those who spoke out against discrimination frequently were fired from their jobs; some were evicted from their homes.

In the 1950s, Baker headed south to help with the formation and organization of SCLC. SCLC was founded

Cambridge mayor Calvin Mowbray. At this meeting, the Treaty of Cambridge was signed, ending the violence and calling for a complete overhaul of the city's race relations. Despite the treaty, the town remained segregated when politicians forced it to a referendum, meaning they would vote on whether or not to abide by it. Richardson "took the controversial step of calling for a boycott of the referendum—even though the civil rights side may have been able to win—arguing that, 'A first-class citizen does not plead to the white power structure to give him something that the whites have no power to give or take away. Human rights are human rights, not white rights.'"[2]

Richardson was praised for her leadership and role in the Cambridge movement and is credited with influencing the later Black Power movement, which was more militant in its efforts to achieve rights and respect for black people. Like Ella Baker, Richardson was not content with slow and steady progress and was committed to doing whatever it took to achieve her goals.

Gloria Richardson (front, center) remained fearless and stood by her beliefs even when she faced violence.

1. Quoted in Black Girl with Long Hair, "The Story Behind This Iconic Image of a Black Woman Pushing Aside a National Guardsman's Bayonet," BGLH Marketplace, January 10, 2017. bglh-marketplace. com/2017/01/the-story-behind-this-iconic-image-of-a-black-woman-pushing-aside-a-national-guardsmans-bayonet/.

2. Quoted in Black Girl with Long Hair, "The Story Behind This Iconic Image."

in January 1957 by King and a number of other southern black ministers. Its primary purpose was to coordinate and support nonviolent forms of direct action, such as boycotts. Baker became SCLC's first full-time staff member. She was asked to coordinate the organization's Crusade for Citizenship, a series of citizen education programs designed to promote voter registration. She managed to organize church rallies in 22 cities, but there was no follow-up to the rallies from the SCLC leadership. The SCLC ministers were more focused, at that time, on their own churches and ministries and did not want to take the time to recruit voters or teach them how to vote, so the plan for local registration never got off the ground.

The failure of the ministers to follow through with voter registration was just one example of Baker's frustration with the leadership. She frequently challenged the male leadership and male dominance within that organization and others. While she respected King, she also had serious differences of opinion with him that she was not hesitant about voicing.

Baker believed that national leaders should draw their strength from ordinary people, not from the media or powerful financial backers, as King seemed to do at times. She once stated, "I have always thought what is needed is the development of people who are interested not in being leaders as much as in developing leadership among other people."[60]

Baker also was frustrated that the ministers who were in charge of SCLC were apparently more interested in making King a national icon than they were in doing actual work for voter registration. She stated,

I have always felt it was a handicap for oppressed people to depend so largely upon a leader, because unfortunately in our culture, the charismatic leader usually becomes a leader because he has found a spot in the public limelight ... There is also the danger in our culture that because a person is called upon to give public statements and is acclaimed by the established, such a person gets to the point of believing that he is the movement. Such people get so involved with playing the game ... that they ... don't do the work of actually organizing people.[61]

Some SCLC insiders and historians believe that King treated Baker more like a secretary than an organizer. They claim that Baker was never given credit for the work she did and that King often refused to take her calls. He and the other ministers seldom listened to her advice about grassroots organizing. Her suggestions, for instance, for greater emphasis on local organizing were largely ignored. Baker said, "I knew from the beginning that as a woman, an older woman, in a group of ministers who are accustomed to having women largely as supporters, there was no place for me to have come into a leadership role."[62]

Although Baker was not given an official leadership role in SCLC, she led in many different ways. She led by example and always advocated for equality, pushed for inclusion of all people in the civil rights movement, encouraged others to join the movement, and treated others with respect and appreciation. In addition, Baker led through her ability to organize various groups of people to fight for an end to discrimination in both small and large ways.

Inspiring Students

From her position within SCLC, Baker watched with great interest as the student sit-ins at lunch counters began in 1960. These protests, undertaken by college students, challenged all-white lunch counters and restaurants. Black students sat down at the counters and refused to leave until they were served—even when white customers harassed them by threatening them with violence or pouring condiments on them. The movement spread throughout the South and succeeded in integrating several department store lunch counters.

Baker knew that the various student groups would be more effective if they were connected and organized. It was for that reason that she arranged a youth conference at Shaw University between April 16 and 18, 1960, which

more than 200 students attended. The male SCLC leaders wanted the students to join their organization and form a student wing. However, Baker had grown quite discouraged with the major civil rights groups and their slow pace of change and accomplishment. Most of the groups were fine with simply speaking out; Baker felt more direct action, such as the sit-ins, was needed. For this reason, she encouraged the students to form their own independent organization instead of joining SCLC or other groups.

In large part because of Baker's advice, the students formed SNCC and declared themselves independent of any established civil rights group. They promised to dedicate themselves to direct action, such as protests and demonstrations. SNCC quickly became a leading civil rights organization as the students began working on voter registration and other issues. In doing so, the student organization moved to the forefront of the civil rights movement; it was the only group that was out in the community, actively working with masses of black people to make positive changes.

Baker eventually left SCLC and became the primary mentor and adviser to SNCC. Inspired by Baker's words and philosophy, many of the young

Lunch counter sit-ins such as this one were largely organized by students. They stayed at the counter even though they knew they would not receive service.

SNCC leaders modeled themselves after her, following her principles of grassroots action. Baker explained, "My sense of it has always been to get people to understand that in the long run they themselves are the only protection they have against violence or injustice ... People have to be made to understand that they cannot look for salvation anywhere but to themselves."[63] She advocated a form of group-centered leadership; she believed that a leader was only a facilitator—someone who could bring out the potential in others. Furthermore, she thought that it was the thousands of ordinary people marching and protesting that helped make the civil rights movement a success.

In her role as the SNCC adviser, Baker met frequently with the student leaders. She also wrote many of the organization's early documents and was on hand to advise the young people on direct action strategy and goals. SNCC leader John Lewis described Baker's advice by writing, "Baker, herself ... praised our success

STUDENT LEADER

Diane Nash was one student who played a crucial leadership role during the civil rights movement. A Northerner by birth, Nash went south to attend Fisk University in Nashville, Tennessee. Appalled by the racism she experienced, she began attending workshops focused on nonviolent forms of protest.

Nash became a prominent member of the Nashville Student Movement and played a pivotal role during the 1960 lunch counter sit-ins that swept the South. Journalist David Halberstam explained Nash's leadership role, writing, "Whatever it was that needed to be done, she just did it. The leader had to be a person who made good decisions under terrible pressure. Like it or not, she was that person."[1] After a confrontation with the mayor on the courthouse steps, Nash and the students were successful in desegregating a number of Nashville lunch counters.

Nash also played a critical role during the 1961 Freedom Rides that challenged interstate bus segregation. When violence stopped the original riders, the Nashville branch of SNCC stepped in. Nash spoke for the students about the reason for continuing the rides when she said, "I strongly felt that the future of the [civil rights] movement was going to be cut short if the Freedom Ride had been stopped as a result of violence. The impression would have been that whenever a movement starts, all you have to do is attack it with massive violence and the blacks will stop."[2]

Nash took on the job of coordinating the group's participation in the rides. She oversaw the recruitment of students to take up the ride, gained support from other civil rights organizations, and became the liaison between the students and the press. When the riders were arrested in Jackson, Mississippi, Nash also kept track of each person who was sent to prison and sent out emergency calls for more riders. In all, more than 300 individuals responded to Nash's call. The Freedom Rides resulted in the integration of all interstate buses and bus facilities.

1. David Halberstam, *The Children*. New York, NY: Fawcett, 1998, p. 144.

2. Quoted in Henry Hampton and Steve Fayer, *Voices of Freedom: An Oral History of the Civil Rights Movement from the 1950s Through the 1980s*. New York, NY: Bantam, 1990, p. 82.

so far but warned that our work had just begun. Integrating lunch counters in stores already patronized by blacks was one thing. Breaking down barriers in areas as racially and culturally entrenched as voting rights, education, and the workplace was going to be much tougher than what we had faced so far."[64]

A Continuing Tradition

Today, Baker's legacy lives on; students of color are just as active as they were in the 1960s. In 2015, a group of students formed to protest racial injustice at the University of Missouri, calling itself Concerned Students 1950 (1950 was the first year black students were admitted to the university). The group had several complaints, but the main one was "charges of persistent racism, particularly complaints of racial epithets [insults] hurled at the student body president, who is black ... along with complaints that the administration did not take the problem seriously enough."[65] After multiple protests, including the threat of a boycott of the university's football team, the president of the university resigned and the chancellor of the Columbia campus took a less powerful job within the university.

This victory is just one example of the power a group of organized students can hold. According to the website Vox, "When black students took over administration buildings and held sit-ins at colleges in the late 1960s, they left change behind them: black studies majors, promises of increased student and faculty diversity, new financial aid programs. Today's protestors are picking up those half-finished fights and demanding universities return to that era's unfulfilled promises."[66] In the 21st century, black student groups have spoken out against things such as Confederate monuments on college campuses, officials' dismissal of students' complaints of racist behavior against them, and underrepresentation of black students and faculty at major universities. This is sometimes a difficult fight in an era where many white people see racism as a problem of the past.

College students are not the only ones getting involved in the fight for racial justice. In the wake of highly visible racially charged incidents, middle and high school students have started their own protests to address things such as police brutality, gun violence, and school closings in predominately black communities. Black girls have led many of these protests. For instance, in March 2019, students at Charlottesville High School in Virginia "walked out of classes ... to demand racial justice less

In 2018, students from Boston, Massachussetts, walked out of class and sat in the hallway in front of the mayor's office to protest multiple issues, including gun violence and homelessness, but focusing mainly on the proposed closure of two Boston public schools. The protestors stated that closing those schools would disproportionately affect students of color.

than a week after a racist online threat shuttered [closed] schools across the city."[67] The walkout was led by the high school's Black Student Union and its president, senior Zyahna Bryant. She explained to the *Washington Post* that, rather than focusing on the threat itself, the students wanted the community to "address the 'whole systems and whole institutions' that perpetuate inequality ... The students issued 10 demands that included calls for leaders in the 4,300-student school system to denounce racism against black and brown students, hire more black teachers and overhaul student discipline policies,"[68] which disproportionately affect students of color. In response to the walkout, the Charlottesville school system began addressing the students' concerns, showing that an organized group of passionate students can have just as much power today as they did in the past.

CHAPTER SEVEN
REGISTERING VOTERS

Many people today believe their vote does not count. They think the vote of one single person will not make any difference. However, the proof that this is untrue is in how hard white people tried to prevent black people from voting even after they legally received the right to do so. Whites were afraid that if blacks turned up at the polls, they would be able to influence the laws in ways that made them equal to whites and could elect politicians who would help promote their advancement in society. Black people were also aware that they had this power, which is why voter registration drives were a central part of the civil rights movement.

The black women of Mississippi did not take a back seat to anybody in their determination to end segregation. They were out front, leading voter registration drives, forming a new political party, and helping create a grassroots revolution that eventually led to thousands of black people becoming civil rights activists. Leading the way was former sharecropper Fannie Lou Hamer.

Getting Involved

Fannie Lou Townsend, the youngest of 20 children, was born in 1917 and raised in Mississippi. Her parents were sharecroppers. Sharecropping was a system in which workers, the vast majority of whom were black, were allowed to live on a plantation in return for working the land. When the crop was harvested, they split the profits with the white plantation owner. However, sharecroppers were required to pay for the seeds and fertilizer out of their half of the proceeds, leaving most of them in constant debt. Fannie Lou continued to work as a sharecropper herself after her marriage to Perry "Pap" Hamer in 1944.

Sharecroppers such as this Mississippi couple generally lived in poverty their whole lives because the sharecropping system was set up to keep them in debt to the white landowners.

Before 1962, Hamer had never heard of the civil rights movement. She attended her first civil rights rally that year after hearing about the meeting at church. Members of SNCC were in town hoping to recruit local black people and register voters. At the rally, Hamer listened closely to what the speakers were saying. "Until then," she later stated, "I didn't know that Negroes could register and vote."[69] She was so impressed with what the young people from SNCC were saying about her rights as a citizen that, along with 16 others, she volunteered to try to register to vote at the county seat of Indianola, Mississippi.

On August 31, 1962, Hamer and the other volunteers rode a bus to Indianola, where they took the literacy test that was required in order to vote in Mississippi. However, they all failed the test. Hamer vowed to keep returning until she passed the test.

Hamer lost her job and home because of this attempt to register to vote. When she returned home, the owner of the plantation where Hamer sharecropped told her that if she was going to try to register to vote, she would have to get off his land. Hamer refused to back down, so the owner followed through with his threat; she was fired from her job and evicted from her home. While her husband stayed behind to help finish the harvest, Hamer left the same day, staying that night with friends. From that day forward, she and her family were constantly threatened and harassed by whites.

Despite the threats, Hamer fully committed herself to civil rights activism. Because of her determination to register and her enthusiasm for fighting racism, Hamer was hired by SNCC in 1962 to work with people in her local area and soon became a major voice in the South. Civil rights activist John Lewis wrote of her, "From that summer on Fannie Lou became a tireless voice for our cause, putting herself out front as an organizer, a speaker ... always an outspoken image of a poor, black woman who was simply out of patience ... Without her and hundreds of women like her, we would never have been able to achieve what we did."[70]

Targeted for Violence

As part of her continuing civil rights activism, Hamer attended a Citizenship School program in Charleston, South Carolina. On June 9, 1963, Hamer, Annell Ponder, June Johnson, and four others were on their way home to Greenwood, Mississippi. Their bus stopped in Winona, Mississippi, and the group walked into the white section of the depot waiting room. There they were approached by several police officers who ordered them to leave the area. When the women refused to do so, they were arrested.

Once at the Winona jail, the women were violently beaten while being questioned. Johnson, a 16-year-old, was hit on the back of the head with a police weapon called a nightstick; Ponder was repeatedly knocked to the floor and emerged from her questioning bloody and bruised. While the other women were being beaten, Hamer overheard the policemen talking about throwing their dead bodies into the Big Black River, where they would never be found.

Hamer described what happened when it was her turn to be questioned: "Three white men came into my room. One was a state highway policeman ... They said they were going to make me wish I was dead."[71] The policemen gave a black prisoner a blackjack—a leather-covered club—and told him to beat Hamer. She later said, "The Negro beat me until he was exhausted ... then the second Negro was given the blackjack ... then the white man started to beat me in the head."[72] Hamer suffered permanent kidney damage and a blood clot that made her blind in the left eye. Additionally, according to historian Taylor Branch, "Hamer was beaten until the fingers protecting her head were blue and the skin on her back swelled up hard as a bone."[73]

Fortunately, the group had left a detailed itinerary before they left on the bus so other civil rights activists would know where they were. When the group did not arrive in Greenwood, their colleagues began making phone calls and finally located the women in

Winona. Lawrence Guyot, a member of SNCC, drove to the jail to try to help the women but was immediately arrested and beaten. Eventually, two SCLC officials were able to arrange for the prisoners' release.

If the authorities in Mississippi believed that such beatings and arrests would stop Hamer and the other civil rights activists, they were very wrong. In June 1964, for instance, Hamer stated, "We're tired of all this beatin', we're tired of takin' this. It's been a hundred years [since the Emancipation Proclamation declared an end to slavery] and we're still bein' beaten and shot at, crosses are still being burned because we want to vote. But I'm goin' to stay in Mississippi and if they shoot me down, I'll be buried here."[74]

Getting Out the Vote

Much of the work that Hamer and other activists performed was aimed at increasing black voter registration. A presidential election was held in 1964, and the civil rights organizations wanted black voters to have a voice in choosing the next president. At that time, black citizens were routinely denied their legal right to vote and therefore did not participate in the election process.

Presidential candidates are elected through a complicated process. Briefly, caucuses are meetings of select members of a political party, during which the attendees decide which candidate to support; primaries allow voters to pick the candidate. The state then selects delegates to attend the national party convention in order to vote for the candidate that has been selected. The presidential candidate for each party is decided by a majority vote of the delegates; this candidate then picks a vice presidential candidate.

In November, citizens vote. The president is determined not by the popular vote, but by the Electoral College. Each state is given the number of electors equivalent to that state's number of members in Congress. A state's electoral vote is based on the popular vote in that state; in other words, if the Republican candidate receives the most votes in Tennessee, then Tennessee's 11 electoral votes would go to the Republican candidate. A majority of electoral votes is needed to elect a president.

In 1964, Mississippi's delegation to the Democratic convention did not include even one black person. Black activists in that state did not believe this delegation fairly represented the thousands of black people who lived in Mississippi, especially since these delegates did not support the civil rights movement. Many whites were

LOCAL VOLUNTEERS MAKE A DIFFERENCE

Amelia Boynton was an Alabama civil rights activist who played a critical role in involving SNCC and SCLC in the politics of Selma, Alabama. Like Fannie Lou Hamer in Mississippi, Boynton worked efficiently at the local level in Alabama. She was, for instance, instrumental in persuading SNCC to make Selma—which had a high level of white supremacy—a center of protest activity for black voter registration. As early as the 1930s, Amelia and her husband, Sam Boynton, became active in the Dallas County Voters League, working to get black citizens registered to vote. Despite their efforts, only 180 black people in the county were registered by 1963 due to barriers thrown up by the city, county, and state.

Boynton also formally invited Martin Luther King Jr. to make Selma a major site for SCLC's stalled voting rights campaign. In January 1965, Boynton was finally successful in persuading King to make Selma his next big campaign stop. Her insurance agency later served as SCLC headquarters.

To further the efforts to register black voters and to highlight the racism in Alabama, King proposed a Selma-to-Montgomery march to take place on March 7, 1965. With King in Atlanta, Georgia, the procession was led by SNCC

determined to maintain the status quo of white economic and political domination; in fact, the delegates had already decided not to support the Democratic candidate, President Lyndon B. Johnson, who favored civil rights legislation.

Black activists, including Hamer, decided to challenge the all-white delegation. In part to bring attention to the problems faced by thousands of disenfranchised black people in the state and the brutality that black people everywhere faced on a daily basis, these activists decided to form a new political party.

In 1964, Hamer was among those who helped found the Mississippi Freedom Democratic Party (MFDP). The members of the MFDP hoped to gain recognition from the national party and replace the white party's delegation to the national convention. They also hoped to play a more active role in the political process so they could gain fair

volunteers. At the end of the Edmund Pettus Bridge, the marchers were met by dozens of highway patrolmen and city policemen who attacked the protesters with clubs and other weapons. Boynton, near the front of the line, was hit by several troopers and knocked unconscious. Hundreds of other marchers were injured as well. The photographs from the bridge made national television news and sickened hundreds of thousands of Americans, many of whom decided to head to Selma and join forces with the protesters. Other protests were held in 80 cities. In 2015, on the 50th anniversary of the Selma march, Boynton helped lead a commemorative march alongside President Barack Obama.

Shown here is the commemorative Selma march. Leading the group alongside Barack and Michelle Obama are U.S. Representative John Lewis (second from left) and Amelia Boynton (second from right), both of whom participated in the original march.

representation in the Democratic National Convention.

In June 1964, the MFDP organized a committee that established countywide and statewide conventions to select their own delegates for the upcoming Democratic National Convention in Atlantic City, New Jersey. More than 800 black delegates attended a state convention held in Jackson, Mississippi, in August 1964. Three women were elected to important delegation positions: Victoria Gray served as national committee chairwoman, Hamer was vice chair of the delegation, and Annie Devine was appointed secretary. All three were powerful grassroots organizers. In total, 68 delegates were chosen to attend the national convention.

Making a Powerful Impression

When the MFDP delegation arrived in Atlantic City in late August, its first order of business was to

Shown here is Fannie Lou Hamer giving her famous speech at the 1964 Democratic National Convention.

meet with the convention's credentials committee and present their arguments for being seated as Mississippi's delegation. One by one they told the story of their struggle to win the right to vote. Roy Wilkins of the NAACP testified, as did Martin Luther King Jr. However, according to a 1994 report by NPR, "The most electrifying moment came when Fannie Lou Hamer got up to speak. Hamer, more than anyone, spoke for the sharecroppers and field hands who made up the majority of the Freedom Party."[75]

Hamer's passionate televised appearance before the credential committee brought national attention to the inequality in Mississippi. In her speech, Hamer dramatically recounted her experience in Winona, Mississippi, and the beating she had received. Her speech stunned American television viewers. She ended by saying, "If the Freedom Democratic Party is not seated now, I question America … Is this America? The land of the free and the home of the brave, where we have to sleep with our telephones off the hook because our lives be threatened

Since people of color are disproportionately poorer than the rest of the population, they are among the most affected.

A third type of law affects the process of registering to vote—and staying registered. In many states, a person must register to vote long before the actual election. After 2008, some states that had previously allowed same-day registration eliminated this policy, requiring voters to register months in advance—and, critics say, the process of registering can be confusing, causing people to unknowingly make mistakes and miss the registration deadline. For those who miss the deadline, voting is not an option. The organization Center for American Progress explained how this can contribute to voter suppression:

> In New Hampshire, for example, strict voter registration laws that require those registering within 30 days of an election to prove they live in the ward or town where they are trying to vote were in place on Election Day this year. This requirement disproportionately disadvantaged college students, who number more than 90,000 in a state with a voting-age population of slightly more than one million. In Georgia, 53,000 voter registrants— 70 percent of whom were black— were placed in "pending" status by the secretary of state because of minor misspellings or missing hyphens on their registration forms. A federal judge intervened to stop this practice ... four days before the election—citing the "differential treatment inflicted on a group of individuals who are predominantly minorities." However, those with pending registration statuses were still forced to prove eligibility, including U.S. citizenship, before voting on Election Day, which can be difficult for Americans lacking access to birth certificates, passports, or nationalization documents.[79]

As in the past, black women have been at the forefront of this fight. One example is Stacey Abrams, an American politician who served as the minority leader of the Georgia House of Representatives from 2011 to 2017. In 2018, she was nominated by the Democratic Party as a candidate for governor of Georgia—the first black woman in history to be nominated for the office of governor by a major party. In her campaign, she was particularly outspoken about the topic of voter suppression, vowing to overturn those laws in her state and setting up a helpline for people who encountered problems

Stacey Abrams has been outspoken about her intentions to eliminate voter suppression.

at the polls. Abrams also founded the New Georgia Project, an organization that carries on the tradition of Hamer and other female civil rights leaders by promoting voter registration. She lost the gubernatorial, or state governor, election, but her work inspired thousands of other women to continue to fight voter suppression.

The female civil rights leaders of the past fought injustice in ways big and small, although their amazing achievements were frequently overlooked and few of them became household names. Their courage and dedication laid the groundwork for the civil rights battles that black women continue to fight in the 21st century. Although great progress has been made in many areas, there is still more to do before true equality between black and white Americans is achieved—and black women have shown that they will not rest until this goal is accomplished.

NOTES

Introduction: Women's Work

1. Lynne Olson, *Freedom's Daughters: The Unsung Heroines of the Civil Rights Movement from 1830 to 1970*. New York, NY: Simon & Schuster, 2001, pp. 15–16.
2. Quoted in Olson, *Freedom's Daughters*, p. 251.
3. Quoted in Bettye Collier-Thomas and V.P. Franklin, eds., *Sisters in the Struggle: African American Women in the Civil Rights–Black Power Movement*. New York, NY: New York University Press, 2001, p. 116.
4. Andrew Young, *An Easy Burden: The Civil Rights Movement and the Transformation of America*. New York, NY: Harper Collins, 1996, p. 143.

Chapter One: Fighting to End Lynching

5. "History of Lynchings," NAACP, accessed on May 9, 2019. www.naacp.org/history-of-lynchings/.
6. Quoted in Karenna Gore Schiff, *Lighting the Way: Nine Women Who Changed Modern America*. New York, NY: Hyperion, 2005, p. 2.
7. Quoted in Jennifer McBride, "Ida B. Wells: Crusade for Justice," Webster University, accessed on June 25, 2019. faculty.webster.edu/woolflm/idabwells.html.
8. "History of Lynchings," NAACP.
9. Quoted in Schiff, *Lighting the Way*, p. 19.
10. Quoted in Linda O. McMurry, *To Keep the Waters Troubled: The Life of Ida B. Wells*. New York, NY: Oxford University Press, 1998, p. 139.
11. Quoted in Sanford Wexler, *The Civil Rights Movement: An Eyewitness History*. New York, NY: Facts On File, 1993, p. 23.
12. "Mary Burnett Talbert," National Women's Hall of Fame, accessed on May 9, 2019. www.womenofthehall.org/inductee/mary-burnett-talbert/.
13. "Mary Burnett Talbert," National Women's Hall of Fame.
14. Jamil Smith, "The Exploitation of Lynching," *Rolling Stone*, February 26, 2019. www.rollingstone.com/politics/politics-features/the-exploitation-of-lynching-800423/.

Chapter Two: Organizations for Black Women

15. Quoted in "Ecumenical Leaders Recall Dorothy I. Height as a Tireless Supporter of Church

Unity," National Council of Churches, April 20, 2010. www.ncccusa.org/news/100420height.html.

16. Lea E. Williams, "Dorothy Irene Height: A Life Well-Lived," *Phi Kappa Phi Forum*, July 1, 2011, p. 9.

17. Dorothy Height, *Open Wide the Freedom Gates*. New York, NY: PublicAffairs, 2003, p. 7.

18. Height, *Open Wide the Freedom Gates*, p. 64.

19. Quoted in Height, *Open Wide the Freedom Gates*, p. 115.

20. Quoted in Collier-Thomas and Franklin, *Sisters in the Struggle*, p. 87.

21. Quoted in "Open Wide the Freedom Gates," PBS *NewsHour*, July 17, 2003. www.pbs.org/newshour/show/open-wide-the-freedom-gates.

22. Williams, "Dorothy Irene Height," p. 10.

23. Quoted in "Obama Calls Height a Champion of 'Righteous Cause," *Denver Post*, April 29, 2010. www.denverpost.com/2010/04/29/obama-calls-height-a-champion-of-righteous-cause/.

24. "Our Mission," NACWC, accessed on May 9, 2019. www.nacwc.com/mission.

25. Meg Anderson, "Phyllis Wheatley Women's Clubs (1895-)," BlackPast, May 17, 2009. www.blackpast.org/african-american-history/phyllis-wheatley-womens-clubs-1895/.

Chapter Three: Learning About Citizenship

26. Olson, *Freedom's Daughters*, p. 215.

27. Quoted in Collier-Thomas and Franklin, *Sisters in the Struggle*, p. 103.

28. Quoted in Vicki L. Crawford, Jacqueline Anne Rouse, and Barbara Woods, eds., *Women in the Civil Rights Movement: Trailblazers and Torchbearers*. Bloomington, IN: Indiana University Press, 1993, p. 92.

29. Taylor Branch, *Parting the Waters: America in the King Years: 1954–1963*. New York, NY: Simon & Schuster, 1988, p. 576.

30. Quoted in Jacquelyn Dowd Hall et al., "Their Own Talking: Septima Clark and Women in the Civil Rights Movement," *Southern Cultures*, Summer 2010. www.southerncultures.org/article/i-train-the-people-to-do-their-own-talking-septima-clark-and-women-in-the-civil-rights-movement/.

31. Taylor Branch, *Pillar of Fire: America in the King Years, 1963–1965*. New York, NY: Simon & Schuster, p. 70.

32. Hall et al., "Their Own Talking."

33. Mack T. Hines III and Dianne Reed, "Educating for Social Justice: The Life and Times of Septima Clark in Review," *Advancing Women in Leadership*, vol. 22, Winter 2007.

34. Olson, *Freedom's Daughters*, p. 223.

35. Quoted in Olson, *Freedom's Daughters*, p. 224.
36. Schiff, *Lighting the Way*, p. 258.

Chapter Four: Organizing a Life-Changing Boycott

37. Quoted in David Halberstam, *The Fifties*. New York, NY: Fawcett Columbine, 1993, p. 545.
38. Quoted in Kevin Markey, *100 Most Important Women of the 20th Century*. Des Moines, IA: Meredith, 1998, p. 39.
39. Halberstam, *The Fifties*, p. 541.
40. Quoted in Donnie Williams and Wayne Greenhaw, *The Thunder of Angels: The Montgomery Bus Boycott and the People Who Broke the Back of Jim Crow*. Chicago, IL: Lawrence Hill, 2006, pp. 47–48.
41. Quoted in Herb Boyd, *We Shall Overcome*. Naperville, IL: Sourcebooks, 2004, p. 49.
42. Quoted in Wexler, *The Civil Rights Movement*, p. 70.
43. Quoted in Henry Hampton and Steve Fayer, *Voices of Freedom: An Oral History of the Civil Rights Movement from the 1950s Through the 1980s*. New York, NY: Bantam, 1990, p. 23.
44. Quoted in Clayborne Carson, ed., *The Autobiography of Martin Luther King, Jr.* New York, NY: Warner, 1998, p. 66.
45. Quoted in Crawford, Rouse, and Woods, *Women in the Civil Rights Movement*, p. 75.

46. Quoted in Denise L. Berkhalter, "Behind the Boycott," *Crisis*, March/April 2006.
47. David Jackson, "Obama: Rosa Parks' Courage Inspires Us Today," *USA Today*, February 27, 2013. www.usatoday.com/story/news/politics/2013/02/27/obama-rosa-parks-statue-boehner/1950985/.

Chapter Five: Desegregating Schools

48. Quoted in Juan Williams, "Daisy Bates and the Little Rock Nine," NPR, September 21, 2007. www.npr.org/templates/story/story.php?storyId=14563865.
49. Melba Pattillo Beals, *Warriors Don't Cry: A Searing Memoir of the Battle to Integrate Little Rock's Central High*. New York, NY: Washington Square, 1994, p. 33.
50. Daisy Bates, *The Long Shadow of Little Rock: A Memoir*. Fayetteville, AR: University of Arkansas Press, 1986, p. 4.
51. Quoted in Clayborne Carson et al., eds., *Eyes on the Prize: Documents, Speeches, and Firsthand Accounts from the Black Freedom Struggle, 1954–1960*. New York, NY: Viking, 1991, p. 98.
52. Halberstam, *The Fifties*, p. 674.
53. Halberstam, *The Fifties*, p. 689.
54. Lauren Camera, "The New Segregation," *U.S. News & World Report*, July 26, 2016.

www.usnews.com/news/articles/2016-07-26/racial-tensions-flare-as-schools-resegregate.

55. Quoted in Camera, "The New Segregation."

56. Camera, "The New Segregation."

57. Quoted in Jenny Jarvie, "'It Feels Like We're Back in the '60s,'" *Los Angeles Times*, October 22, 2006. www.latimes.com/archives/la-xpm-2006-oct-22-na-deseg22-story.html.

Chapter Six: Student Protests

58. "Who Was Ella Baker?," Ella Baker Center for Human Rights, accessed on July 10, 2019. ellabakercenter.org/about/who-was-ella-baker.

59. Collier-Thomas and Franklin, *Sisters in the Struggle*, p. 10.

60. Quoted in Francesca Polletta, *Freedom Is an Endless Meeting: Democracy in American Social Movements*. Chicago, IL: University of Chicago Press, 2012, p. 63.

61. Quoted in Crawford, Rouse, and Woods, *Women in the Civil Rights Movement*, p. 64.

62. Quoted in Collier-Thomas and Franklin, *Sisters in the Struggle*, p. 188.

63. Quoted in Crawford, Rouse, and Woods, *Women in the Civil Rights Movement*, p. 58.

64. John Lewis and Michael D'Orso, *Walking with the Wind: A Memoir of the Movement*. San Diego, CA: Harcourt Brace & Co., 1998, p. 108.

65. John Eligon and Richard Pérez-Peña, "University of Missouri Protests Spur a Day of Change," *New York Times*, November 9, 2015. www.nytimes.com/2015/11/10/us/university-of-missouri-system-president-resigns.html.

66. Libby Nelson, "A Racial Reckoning on Campuses Is Overdue," Vox, November 11, 2015. www.vox.com/2015/11/11/9716460/missouri-protests-yale-race.

67. Debbie Truong, "Charlottesville Students Walk Out of Class After Racist Threat Closed Schools," *Washington Post*, March 25, 2019. www.washingtonpost.com/local/education/charlottesville-students-walk-out-of-class-after-racist-threat-closed-schools/201/03/25/4eae1a84-4f39-11e9-a3f7-78b7525a8d5f_story.html.

68. Truong, "Charlottesville Students."

Chapter Seven: Registering Voters

69. Quoted in Collier-Thomas and Franklin, *Sisters in the Struggle*, p. 141.

70. Lewis and D'Orso, *Walking with the Wind*, p. 188.

71. Quoted in Schiff, *Lighting the Way*, p. 286.

72. Quoted in Boyd, *We Shall Overcome*, p. 182.

73. Branch, *Parting the Waters*, p. 819.

74. Quoted in Wexler, *The Civil Rights Movement*, p. 207.

75. Lynn Neary, "Special Report on Mississippi Freedom Democrats—1964," *All Things Considered*, NPR, August 27, 1994.

76. Quoted in Peter Dreler, "'I Question America'—Remembering Fannie Lou Hamer's Famous Speech 50 Years Ago," *HuffPost*, last updated December 6, 2017. www.huffpost.com/entry/is-this-america-rememberi_b_5715135.

77. Michael Cooke, "Mississippi Freedom Democratic Party," *Encyclopedia of African-American Culture and History*, 2006. www.encyclopedia.com/history/encyclopedias-almanacs-transcripts-and-maps/mississippi-freedom-democratic-party.

78. "The Facts About Voter Suppression," ACLU, accessed on May 28, 2019. www.aclu.org/facts-about-voter-suppression.

79. Danielle Root and Aadam Barclay, "Voter Suppression During the 2018 Midterm Elections," Center for American Progress, November 20, 2018. www.americanprogress.org/issues/democracy/reports/2018/11/20/461296/voter-suppression-2018-midterm-elections/.

FOR MORE INFORMATION

Books

Adler, David A. *Heroes for Civil Rights*. New York, NY: Holiday House, 2008.
This book focuses on many civil rights leaders, including Fannie Lou Hamer and Rosa Parks.

Devlin, Rachel. *A Girl Stands at the Door: The Generation of Young Women Who Desegregated America's Schools*. New York, NY: Basic Books, 2018.
This detailed history explores school desegregation and the women and girls who led the fight for equal education.

Harness, Cheryl. *Rabble Rousers: Twenty Women Who Made a Difference*. New York, NY: Dutton Children's, 2003.
This book includes short biographies of several influential women, including Sojourner Truth, Ida B. Wells-Barnett, and Fannie Lou Hamer.

Harris, Duchess, and Deirdre Head. *Barbara Jordan: Politician and Civil Rights Leader*. Minneapolis, MN: Core Library, 2019.
Readers learn about Barbara Jordan's work as a political figure, which was instrumental to the civil rights movement.

McWhorter, Diane. *A Dream of Freedom: The Civil Rights Movement from 1954–1968*. New York, NY: Scholastic, 2004.
McWhorter takes an overall look at some of the key moments of the civil rights movement.

Mulholland, Loki, Angela Fairwell, and Charlotta Janssen. *She Stood for Freedom: The Untold Story of a Civil Rights Hero, Joan Trumpauer Mulholland*. Salt Lake City, UT: Shadow Mountain, 2016.
This biography of Joan Trumpauer Mulholland gives the story of her life, from her childhood in 1950s Virginia to her participation in various aspects of the civil rights movement, including the Freedom Rides of 1961.

Websites

Civil Rights Women Leaders of the Carolinas

ncwomenofcivilrights.wordpress.com

This website gives biographical information on three female civil rights leaders who were active in North and South Carolina: Ella Baker, Pauli Murray, and Septima Clark.

NPR: Rosa Parks Interviews

www.npr.org/templates/story/story.php?storyId=4973548

When Rosa Parks died in 2005, NPR compiled two interviews she gave about her involvement in the Montgomery bus boycott.

PBS: Leaders of the Civil Rights Movement

www.pbs.org/black-culture/explore/civil-rights-leaders

This website showcases videos and articles from various PBS documentaries about civil rights leaders.

The Rise and Fall of Jim Crow

www.thirteen.org/wnet/jimcrow

Learn more about how slavery and segregation impacted every aspect of black Americans' lives.

We Shall Overcome

www.nps.gov/nr/travel/civilrights

This project of the National Park Service includes a list of key sites, including places where historic events took place during the civil rights movement and places where leading activists lived, and an interactive map.

INDEX

PICTURE CREDITS

ABOUT THE AUTHOR

Jennifer Lombardo earned her BA in English from the University at Buffalo and still resides in Buffalo, New York, with her cat, Chip. She has helped write a number of books for young adults, on topics ranging from world history to body image. In her spare time, she enjoys cross-stitching, hiking, and volunteering with Habitat for Humanity.